MAD WORLD

a collection of short stories

LAWRENCE BENSON

Miras Press   Minneapolis

MAD WORLD: A collection of short stories.

Published by Miras Press, PO Box 581671
Minneapolis, Minnesota
55458.

ISBN: 0-9823569-0
ISBN-13: 978-0-9823569-0-6

www.miraspress.com

To my mother—
see...healing is possible.

ACKNOWLEDGEMENTS

When I was considering these words, who to thank regarding the possibility and actuality of this manuscript, two themes arose: reflection and healing. Reflection, in the cognitive sense of 'thinking about' relative to one's Self, is a process that I hope all who engage these stories experience, including the perils of daring to view a representation of one's face in the imagination via a reflective surface. Because of my inability to connect "me" to my own face in a mirror[1], and my inability to connect to the mimetic one presented by my father, I turned to glimpses of my Self in others, specifically, those willing to expose the inevitable vulnerability of existence. This is where healing begins, because concomitant with this recognition is the reconnection to the wound—the disconnection: from our "Selves", our bodies, and each other. The reconnection is a process of contextualizing and re-contextualizing that ultimately places the possibility of a "real" Self before another "real" Self as a test of existence. I have encountered these brave people from Frederica, Delaware to Portland, Oregon with chance meetings in Bozeman, Montana and Wheeling, West Virginia among other places. In some of my most lonely moments, strangers' faces seemed the closest representation to my own face that I could recognize. I am grateful to them all; however, special acknowledgment is necessary for those who went above and beyond, those who helped me heal and who have endured. Thank you Ezra Hale and Suzanne Lavelle-Foley for your support and love through my most and least proud moments, for providing an opportunity for me to see myself and the characteristics to which I aspire, and for the scarce times when we let go and the moment overwhelms us with the Present.

---

[1] I cover this poetically in <u>The Secret Confessions of Muscle: Excerpts from the Fascia Diaries</u>.

Thanks to Georgia Afton, Ann Forsties, Beth Gedatus, Kathleen Keller, Marie Malinowski, and Marc Thompson for helping create a safe environment for me and my work to grow.

The staff and faculty of Hamline University's MFA Program, and to my fellow classmates who have shared their lives, talent, and open minds over the years—many thanks as well.

Special thanks to Judith Katz, Deborah Keenan, and Sheila O'Connor for their guidance of these stories.

Thank you, John Loveland, for opening yourself to my love—and, ultimately, Love—without which this book would not be possible.

And to my family, thanks for the tumultuous ride that was, is, and will become my life, and for planting the seeds of my personality, inclinations, mood, empathy, and sentience.

TABLE OF CONTENTS

Bring it to me, your rage
gently
to soothe the burn
calm the swelling that grows
beneath the skin, puss
of a heartless tyrannical nation.

Falling reigns brash and untrue
like stories of savagery and inferiority
all because of my ebony.

My hands bleed
when I attempt to grab them,
the falling rains
soothe my rage.

The Wetness is welcome.

MAD WORLD

A collection of short stories

Canons scream at the tops of their lungs and pierce the ears of the horrible world with no mercy. A head...

RESPECTIVE BLUES

July 23rd, 1968. Tuesday. Reported temperature: one-hundred and ten degrees. The small town of Helluva, Alabama. One-hundred and fifty miles east of Birmingham. Despite race-riots the previous summer in Newark and Detroit, burning crosses, and nonviolent marches that had sometimes turned brutal, Helluva had managed to keep a little of the peace, mainly because almost all of the Blacks lived in the country outside of town. There were only two Black families in the town proper, and they were mostly left alone. These families had long histories in town, back to its settlement, and were tolerated in the community. They had never caused any problems, but during such a volatile time, worsened by increasing civil unrest concerning the Vietnam War, their livelihoods and their very lives seemed always at stake. There were a few White folks in Helluva who felt that the "nigger" families should be run out, their property and assets sold at auction or simply looted. Some of them even spoke openly about Dr. Martin Luther King, Jr.'s murder a few months earlier—that, somehow, he had deserved to die for stirring up so many problems. The few trouble-makers would occasionally flare up; go on hate sprees and attack: corner the Blacks wherever they could, shout slurs and innuendos about their bodies, their humanness, and subsequently, their right to exist any further. They were loosely organized: White, teenage boys unknowingly incited by their parents' secret loathing of themselves, and fear that Helluva would, too, soon erupt. There were not many cases of actual violence because others in town would find out and shine a spotlight on their hate. Weeks earlier, in response to a supposed burglary by one of the two Black boys in town, "Coon," "Go back to Africa," and "Die Nigger Die!" appeared on his family's home in black spray-paint. Mostly, there was a lot of cussing, spitting, and pushing. However, some of these incidences got out of hand, heated, and escalated quickly. Such is the case with Frank Myers, Jr.

Frank Myers, Jr. was a freshly-turned sixteen year-old boy from new money. His father, the town's high-powered lawyer, came from what was known as 'dirt farmers,' had worked hard in the fields and in school to get off of his family's turnip farm. His father had earned a football scholarship to the University of Alabama, but then turned his sights to civil rights law when his body failed him during his sophomore year. Frank Myers Sr. was well-respected, even in the Big City, and he wore his position in the community with cautious pride. Frank Jr. looked more like his mother: medium frame, evenly tanned skin, thick auburn hair, full lips, and wide brown eyes. He smiled softly like her, too. He was a nerd: he took calculus and physics, entered and won almost every science fair he could, and spent hours with his face buried in *Popular Mechanics* and *Science World*. His closest friend was Jeffrey Toms, a junior who had just officially lost his title as 'The New Guy'. Frank Jr. was a decent tennis player (he had said it was because of the physics and math involved), and that, plus his family's reputation, had saved him from a childhood of ass-kickings and wedgies.

Frank Jr. got up around six that morning to play tennis before it got unbearably hot. That July had been one of the warmest on record, averaging temperatures of ninety-four degrees. He had wanted to compete for the first singles spot on the team; he knew he would have to work his one-hand backhand, get more 'zip' on his serve to beat Chauncey Hamilton. He practiced at the outdoor high school courts that had recently been remodeled after both the boys' and girls' teams placed top three in Regionals for the first time. Big things were expected from the teams, and Frank Jr. was determined to play a large part in this success.

He usually practiced his ground strokes against the hitting wall and then worked on his serve. By that time, someone would show up to hit with, and possibly play a set or two before it got too hot. Mostly, he wound up playing with Jeffrey, who had been first singles at his school before he moved to Helluva two years ago. He was now second singles, behind Chauncey and in front of Frank Jr. However, Jeffrey seemed satisfied with his position on the team, and had told Frank Jr. he would never challenge for first singles because he just loved to play tennis. There was an obvious division on the team: Chauncey's crew: Robert, Kirk, and Phil—then everybody else. They rarely came to the courts because Chauncey had a court in his backyard. That day, when Frank Jr. finished his serves and waited, he spotted Chauncey and his crew pulling into the parking lot. He watched them unload their gear and head down the path towards the tennis courts.

"Hey, Frankie, baby! Introduce us to your new friends," said Chauncey, looking around the empty space behind and to the side of Frank Jr. The others chuckled dutifully.

"Yeah, that's real funny, a laugh riot," he said, eyeing the stooges with Chauncey.

"No, really, I thought you usually hit with Jeffrey?"

"Yeah, I don't know where he is. He's usually here by now. I think I'm just gonna hit a few more serves then take off. How come you're not playin' at *your* house?"

"I thought I'd come down here and see how the common folk are livin'," said Chauncey, prompting his gang to snickers. "Why don't you stay and hit with us, it's only nine o'clock."

"Nah. It's already pretty hot and its supposed to get the hottest it's been all summer."

"Come on, I'll even play you myself, beat up on you a little bit. It's been awhile and I don't want you to forget what it feels like."

The crowd busted out in a chorus of "ooohs," "damns" and "ouches."

"Yeah, I think I'm gonna cut out."

"Well, maybe you better go then. I guess your ass-whuppin' can wait."

Frank Jr. shook his head and looked at Chauncey. He noticed the sweat on Chauncey's face, how it coated his surprisingly pale skin, dripped down the sides along his blonde hairline. It was hotter and there was a sense of subtle escalation that made Frank Jr. uneasy. He tried to push past Chauncey and his gang, but they formed a wall and blocked his every step. Finally, he stopped and stared at Chauncey. There was now more sweat on both of them, and the collars of their shirts had changed to a darker, damper shade of their respective blues.

"Frank Jr.!" A loud voice barreled from the path's direction. They all turned to see Jeffrey emerging from the top of the hill. "Let's go, man!"

Frank Jr. began walking then Chauncey stepped in front of him. They stared at each other, and then Frank Jr. shouldered past, cautiously nudging Chauncey aside. When he reached Jeffrey at the top of the hill, Jeffrey turned and presented Chauncey and his crew the finger.

"We should fuck up his car," said Jeffrey.

* * *

It was official. The record had been broken. One-hundred and fifteen degrees. No one in Helluva could recall a time when it was hotter, when people wanted out of their skin as much. Air-conditioners and fans droned in overtime, and people guzzled iced tea, water, and lemonade by the pitcher. Some passed out on the spot because of the severe heat. Others were rushed to the emergency room due to dehydration and varying cases of heatstroke. There was a report of an elderly man dying in his car, and garbage collection included picking up dead stray animals that, in the continued sweltering heat, had begun to quickly decompose.

Frank Jr. had said goodbye to Jeffrey at the school, and then drove back to his house where he found himself lamenting over his confrontation with Chauncey. He had always backed down from fights, not because he couldn't fight or was afraid to fight, but because he had been taught that fighting is for people who are out of control of themselves. Frank Jr. wanted and needed to be in control, and those moments, like that one with Chauncey, made him feel small and insignificant, the way his father could with one simple look. Whenever he felt himself heating up, his anger rising, he imagined his father's eyes and the subsequent shame that would overtake him if he were to get into a brawl. When he got home, he took off all of his clothes except his boxers, laid in front of the air-conditioner that, like most others in town, was on the verge of breaking down as the result of being overworked. After resorting to three fans blowing directly on him, and limitless glasses of iced tea, he decided to go for a swim. He went out to the pool, took off his underwear, and then dove in. The water was warm even with the pool's cooling system. However, anything was better than the harsh, swelling heat.

* * *

He began to feel like he was boiling. As he was getting out of the pool, to head back to his retreat between the fans, there was a loud stutter then a bang, like a car had backfired, was on its last leg. However, he knew exactly what it was—the air-conditioner had finally died, succumbed to the overbearing heat and its inability to self-regulate. The poolside thermometer had long since maxed-out at one-hundred degrees, and it was barely eleven o'clock. He got out of the pool and didn't bother to cover himself with a towel. He walked, dripping with water and sweat, to the family room where the fans were whirring,— the noise, not the relief from heat, being the most noticeable and annoying. He pointed the fans towards the center of the room and then stretched out on the floor between them.

"Fuckin' Chauncey!" he yelled, into the hot, open air, and then rolled onto his stomach. He managed to briefly doze off in the unbearable heat, but awoke to the feeling of no longer being the only person in the room.

"Frank Jr., please put something on to cover yourself. I know it's hot, but we are still decent people." His mother walked through with a brown-paper shopping bag that seemed to be sweating as its bottom darkened.

"What's in the bag?" Frank Jr. got up, grabbed a towel from the couch, and then wrapped himself.

"Maybe the last semi-frozen ice-cream in the county. Hurry up with some bowls while the gettin' is good."

He grabbed bowls out of the cupboard and spoons from the silverware drawer. His mother lifted the melting half-gallon of his favorite Blue Bell chocolate ice-cream out of the bag. Light brown drops trickled down the sides of the container and her bare arm. She placed the carton in the sink then licked her fingers. Frank Jr. dispensed with the bowl and dug in with his spoon. He handed a spoon to his mother and she followed suit. They smiled at each other and ate faster, trying to enjoy the ever so subtle coolness of the rapidly melting ice-cream.

"Lynette will be here around four to clean the house. I'm going to Miss Ella's to get my hair rolled and set, to the cleaner's if they haven't closed, and then back to the market. I should be home by five, so try to be clothed when she gets here, and try not to make even more of a mess, okay?"

"You're still havin' the party?"

"Yes, *we* are. Eight o'clock *sharp*."

"Even after what happened today? That gunfight in Ohio with the cops and Mr. Evans' group?"

"So, you heard about Fred?" she said, stopping mid-scoop.

"Everybody's talkin' about it. It's all over the TV news. They're callin' it the Glenville Shootout. Is he dead?"

"I don't know, Honey. That's all the more reason to have this party. It's really important to your father. A lot of his law colleagues and some other very influential people who can help the Cause will be here."

"In this heat? Without AC? That's gonna blow."

"Watch your language…and it won't. Lynette's nephew, Paul, is driving here to hopefully fix the air-conditioner. You remember Paul don't you? I guess he's some kind of electronics whiz."

"He dropped her off one time. Why don't you let *me* fix it?"

"Honey, I have no doubt that you can fix it," she said, rubbing her hand on his head. "You can do pretty much anything with wires, but Paul does this for a living. He's doing us a big favor by driving in this heat so that our guests can be comfortable."

"Well, what if I'm not here, or catchin' some z's?"

"You know Lynette has her own key. Just don't make a mess. This is very important to your father."

"I know. You said that already." He kissed her on the cheek then threw his spoon into the other side of the sink. It clanged around, reminded him of the noise in the room, that, to be heard above all the fans on 'high', they had been almost yelling.

* * *

Frank Jr. was in the shower when the phone rang. He wrapped a towel around his waist then ran to the phone-stand in the hall.

"Hello?"

" . . . "

"Jeffrey!

" . . . "

"Just takin' a cool shower."

" . . . "

"Yeah, come on over, but my parents are still havin' this party and people are comin' by to clean and stuff, so I can only hang for a little while."

" . . . "

"Four at the latest."

" . . . "

"If you get here by one, that'll be three hours."

" . . . "

"No way, man. I have to be at this party."

" . . . "

"Forget it. My old man would kill me."

" . . . "

"Okay, see you in a flash."

* * *

It had seemed like everything was melting. Plastics withered like unwatered flowers, and the tar smell had intensified by the

heating of the roads in the record heat. For all intent, Helluva
had shut down. Few places had electricity as the overburdened
town succumbed to power outages. Fewer had air-conditioning.
There were still some people out of doors, trying to do everyday
chores with grace and fortitude. Most others rode around
with their windows rolled up tightly and air-conditioners
blasting. They drove slowly to save gas; their faces took on
an eerie, blue-grayness from the artificial cold, like the tone
beneath a snowy TV channel. Jeffrey pulled up in a tan Pontiac
GTO, windows rolled down, shirtless, blaring *Born to be
Wild*.

"Turn it down!" Frank Jr. said, running towards the driveway.
"And park in back."

Jeffrey began to back up when a silver and black Triumph pulled
in behind him. The driver laid on the horn until Chauncey got
out of the passenger-side door holding two six-packs of Pabst
Blue Ribbon.

"Hey, Ladies!"

Frank Jr. glared at Jeffrey. Jeffrey shrugged his shoulders.

"Hey, Man, I know, but it's really hot and they have beer. *Cold*
beer."

"Yeah, lighten up Frankie, baby! I was just goofin' earlier at
the courts. Everything's cool. And hey, Jeffrey said your folks
aren't even at your pad, right? So, have a cold one on me. Think
fast."

He tossed a beer to Frank Jr.; Frank Jr. caught it and cut his
eyes at Jeffrey.

"Okay, but only for a few hours. My parents are havin' this important party tonight and Lynette's comin' by to clean. My mom will flip if the house isn't spotless. Park around back."

Three of Chauncey's crew got out of the car holding six-ers of Pabst in each hand. As the driver backed up, he yelled, "We got whisky, too!"

* * *

All seven of the boys sat shirtless in a rough circle, in the living room between the fans, among dozens of beer cans. They passed around a three-quarters empty, 1.75l bottle of Johnny Walker Red.

"Hey, Frankie, baby! Where's the grub around this hell-hole?"

"Hey, Chauncey, it's in the fuckin' kitchen, where do you think it is you nosebleed?"

"Well, go and get us somethin' asshole. It's almost two hours past lunchtime, and we're the guests."

"Uninvited guests…with booze!"

"I figured hospitality is lackin' here on the other side of the tracks."

Chauncey got up then headed towards the kitchen. Frank Jr. tossed a beer can in the air and smashed it like a serve into Chauncey's back.

"Frankie, baby, where's the bread?" yelled Chauncey from the kitchen.

"It's…fuck it, I'm on it." Frank Jr. got up slowly from the floor and then stumbled towards the kitchen.

"Hey, maybe we should go swimming," said Chauncey, as he carelessly spread mayonnaise on a slice of bread and his hand.

"Our pool's boilin' hot and besides, you didn't bring trunks."

"Come on, Frankie, baby! Who wears a suit in this heat?"

Chauncey began pulling off his shorts.

"Whoa, Man! Wait 'til you get outside."

"What's the matter Frankie, baby? You don't want anybody to see your little weiner?"

Chauncey reached for Frank Jr.'s shorts and tried to pants him, but he only managed to grab the string at the top. He tugged again and Frank Jr. resisted, but this time Frank Jr.'s grip slipped, and then his shorts were down at his ankles.

"Oh, my god, Frankie, baby! I didn't know you cared!"

Frank Jr. blushed and quickly pulled up his shorts.

"Look, Chauncey, don't…"

"We better get back."

* * *

The space between the fans had become littered with t-shirts, beer cans, potato chips, and a little vomit. The pool, though on the verge of boiling, was still a cooler place to be, as the air in the space between the fans had now become thick and musty as well as hot. They seemed to move in slow motion through the water. They were never all in the pool at the same time, as one would, inevitably, overheat on the verge of throwing up. Chauncey climbed out then walked over to Frank Jr. who had taken slight refuge under an oversized, pale blue patio umbrella. He stood in front of Frank Jr. completely naked.

"Hey, Frankie, baby! I'm still hungry. Go make me a sandwich."

"Hey, put on some clothes and get it yourself, I mean, now that you know where everything is."

Chauncey smiled, picked up his shorts, and then headed back towards the house. He stopped at the patio door and turned, still naked, to Frank Jr.

"Hey, Frankie, baby! Are you sure there isn't anything I can get for you?" Laughter erupted from the pool as Chauncey did a little dance with his hips that made his penis jangle, and then he disappeared through the patio door. After about ten minutes, there was a loud crash inside of the house, like something shattering.

"What the hell was that!" Frank Jr. jumped up from his towel then fell over, almost pulling down the umbrella as he instinctively grabbed it for leverage.

"I'll check it out," said Jeffrey, getting out of the pool. "I'm kinda hungry, too." Jeffrey put on his shorts then ran into the house. The others, following his lead, climbed out of the pool, clothed, and then staggered toward the house past Frank Jr. who was on all fours on the brick walkway vomiting into the grass. After a few more heaves, he staggered to his feet, and then to the patio door, where he leaned and breathed heavily, tried to make sense of the scene before him: Chauncey was struggling, in glass from a large broken mirror, with a black man. As Frank Jr. yelled, "Stop!", Chauncey broke free, grabbed the empty whisky bottle off of the coffee table, and then, with the cleanest backhand stroke in the county, hit the man on the right side of his head. The man went to the floor like a newly felled tree, and then Chauncey jumped on top of him, began furiously punching his face.

"Chauncey, stop, Man! Stop!" yelled Frank Jr.

The man managed to push Chauncey off of him with his legs. Chauncey fell into the TV and knocked it to the floor, onto its side; it went dark. The man ran towards the front door.

"Stop that fuckin' nigger!" yelled Chauncey, as he got back up to his feet. The other boys stumbled towards the door kicking over beer cans and bowls of chips. One lunged at the man and tackled him by the waist, to the floor, as the others piled on top of him.

"Get off of him!" sneered Chauncey, as he entered the mound of drunken, half-naked boys, and found the man, restrained. He punched the man's face until the blue-black skin split above the man's left eye and blood appeared, dripped to the collar of his white shirt. The other boys kicked the man hard in the groin as they tripped over his lower body.

Frank Jr. fought his way into the pile. "Paul, are you okay? Get off of him! Get the fuck off of him!" He pushed through and saw Chauncey's hands planted firmly around Paul's neck. Tears streamed down Paul's face as he gasped for air.

"Chauncey, you spaz, get off of him! What the hell are you doin'? Stop! Get off of him!"

Frank Jr. hooked Chauncey around the neck with his right arm and then Chauncey reached up and grabbed Frank Jr.'s arm. They rolled to the left, off of Paul, and wrestled for control as the others fell back to the perimeter in various stages of drunkenness. Someone threw up. Chauncey managed to hold down Frank Jr. with the same move as he did with Paul.

"Whatcha' gonna do now, Frankie, baby?"

"Get the fuck off of me!"

"Why? So you can go make out with your little nigger friend?"

"Fuck you! Get off of me!"

"Hey, Jeffrey! Did your buddy here tell you what happened in the kitchen?"

Frank Jr. squirmed, freed one of his knees from the weight of Chauncey, and then kneed Chauncey in the groin. Chauncey barely winced from the blow. Instead, he climbed higher onto Frank Jr.'s torso, and then began wailing on his face.

"Huh, Frankie, baby? Did you tell him? Huh?"

Frank Jr., in his immobile position, continued trying to evade Chauncey's punches. As he turned his head side to side, he saw Paul lying on the floor, a pool of blood forming by his mouth: from his nose, mouth, and the cut above his eye. Paul's eyes fluttered as he moaned. Frank Jr. released his right arm and punched towards Chauncey's face, but only managed a few blows to his stomach which went almost unnoticed. The other boys stood by urging them on as they continued fighting. Frank Jr.'s face bled from an undetermined place, and blood mingled down to his and Chauncey's bare chests. Jeffrey finally tried to intervene, but the other boys, who were, in fact, Chauncey's friends, restrained him. Chauncey continued delivering punches to Frank Jr.'s face, laughing and mocking him.

"Huh, did you tell him? How about I tell him? Huh, Frankie, baby?"

Frank Jr. stopped resisting Chauncey's blows, and then rested his head on the floor towards Paul. Chauncey, with a bewildered frown, stopped hitting Frank Jr. He rolled off of him, to his knees, and then crawled to his feet; the others stood with flushed, blank gazes. Frank Jr. looked at Paul through his own bloody eyes. He watched for the slightest rise and fall of Paul's chest, and when he saw it, he moved his head towards the others at the patio door. One by one, they grabbed their shirts, looked at Frank Jr., and then turned to leave. Chauncey and Jeffrey remained, but Jeffrey seemed to not want to leave until Chauncey was gone. A car horn blared from the back of the house. Chauncey turned and quietly walked out the door. Jeffrey moved towards Frank Jr., but Frank Jr. turned away from the door where they all had been, where they had all witnessed Chauncey's rage and did nothing. Instead, Jeffrey grabbed a towel and placed it next to Paul's head. The towel immediately began turning red. Frank Jr. slowly settled his gaze on a spot above his head, clear from Paul and Jeffrey, towards the TV on the floor, on its side. In the strange darkness of the blank TV screen, by the light of the still, blazing, late afternoon sun, he saw past the reflection of his damaged, bloody face, through his eyes, into himself, what his life might become from that moment forward. It hurt to cry, but even through the blood, he could taste his salty tears.

...bashes a wall and the wall begins to bleed and cry but no one comes by to give. Voodoo girls and Christian...

THE ANSWER
TO THE BIG QUESTION

He had told her it was okay to put his hands down there 'cause he was her uncle. He got real mad when she told him she didn't want to do it again, too, and he told her don't tell nobody, not even me, her only sister. She didn't remember much about it 'cept his hands was cold and James Brown was singin' on TV in the background. She said she don't remember sound—don't even remember breathin'.

* * *

"Huh?" said Lainey.

"You hear me, *girl?*"

"No, Daddy. I didn't hear you."

"I *said* 'Don't think you gonna be sittin' up on a Saturday in front of that TV set all day. There's work to do 'roun' here and you gonna watch them kids later."

"*So?*"

"*Soooooooooo*, you best get your ass in gear and get out to do what you got to do before I get back and we ready to go to the bar."

"But I want to watch the rest of this."

"You heard me, Elaine. Now cut off that TV and take her with you to dress them kids!"

Lainey turned back to the TV, watched for a little bit more, got up and then turned it off. She got up and turned it right back 'ON' when Daddy shut the door.

* * *

"Elaine didn't do a damn thing today, did she?"

"Look, that's between you and her. I don't know what on *earth* is goin' on with the two of you, but the two of *you* need to fix it. She *is* only fourteen. Be still, child."

"Don't forget you her mother. You 'sposed to make sure she's doin' right."

"A father is supposed to do that too. I'm almost done, now stop squirmin' and hold still."

"Don't forget you was already carryin' her when you was her age. You just make sure she act right, you hear? You *hear*?" He stood like he always did when he was tryin' to scare somebody: arms crossed all tight up at his chest.

"I hear you," Momma said, finishin' the last braid. "Now, get on girl and tell Elaine to get them kids in the car."

* * *

"Your hair looks good."

"I wish you did it, Lainey. Momma braids too tight sometimes, 'specially when she's *distracted*."

"I can loosen 'em up in the car when we get to Marshall's, okay?"

"You think we gonna be there all day?"

"Yup. Just like usual. Let's go before he starts fussin' and carryin' on, gettin' Momma all riled up."

Lainey reached for me that day and we walked to the car swingin' hand in hand. We didn't do that in such a long time.

We pulled up to Marshall's right around lunchtime and parked on the side next to them 'ugly trees', the ones in the shade where they could see us through the little window; hours and hours in that hot car playin' with old white doll babies, singin' to the radio, pickin' at each other, and sleepin'. Daddy never came out 'til it was time to leave. Momma came out from behind them black, spray-painted doors with a tray of food and drinks. Her light-skinned cheeks would be all flushed red, and heat came up from her body and voice, like when her and Daddy was fightin', and like when she sings a solo with the church choir.

"Here, we got hamburgers, french fries, subs and fried chicken. And y'all get your own soda. Elaine, make sure everybody stays in the car…that means you too. And make sure them kids eat before they drink all that soda and make sure they don't make a mess, you *hear*?"

Lainey took a deep breath and let it out through her nose tryin' not to make a sound. Sometimes she made a little pig-snort from her nose and we'd all bust out laughin' and Momma would be like 'Elaine, young ladies don't make noises like that!'—but sometimes she smiled too. One time Lainey made the mistake of askin' when they was gonna be done, and after Momma slapped her 'cross her face, when Lainey was holdin' back tears, Momma told her not to question grown folk about their business.

William musta' seen Lainey before, 'specially since him and Jimmy was good friends, and Jimmy and Lainey real close cousins. She said she saw him around, but never paid him no mind 'til that day him and Jimmy pulled up next to us in Marshall's parkin' lot.

"Elaine, this is William. You know William, right?"

"Why you bein' all proper, *James*?"

"Stop playin', Lainey."

"I seen him around before. How you doin', William?"

"Good. And you?"

"Been better."

Jimmy walked back 'round to the driver's side of his car, bent down, and pulled up a brown, paper bag. He put it up to his lips and took a swig of Tiger Rose; everybody and they brother knew Tiger Rose was Jimmy's drink. He turned on the radio and we all started boppin' aroun'. Jimmy called us over and gave William a head nod to our car. He shot Jimmy that "hold on a minute" sign with his pointy finger. Instead, he opened his door, the passenger side door, and Lainey opened her door, the driver's side door. They smiled at each other and started talkin' across cars. Jimmy finished his whole bottle; we kids fell right on off to sleep. They probably talked the whole time, 'til all the grown folks came out of Marshall's loud and stumblin' in the dark. William already slid Jimmy over to the passenger seat and was revving up the engine. We kids all crawled back in the car with Lainey after Jimmy passed out and the radio station was only static. William and Lainey smiled all big at each other when him and Jimmy pulled out of the driveway. Lainey slid over for Momma to drive. Daddy mumbled somethin' and fell in the backseat with the rest of us kids.

"Who was that boy with Jimmy?"

"That's just William, you know, Jimmy's friend from the Plant? He stays up in Smyrna. He's been aroun' before with Jimmy, don't you remember?"

"Well, whoever he is, you better watch out for him and them other boys too. You *know* they just after one thing."

"We was just talkin'."

"That's all better be goin' on. He's just like all the rest of 'em includin' your drunk, sorry-ass daddy."

Momma looked straight back at Daddy then at Lainey and then right back at the road. Now, she was kinda cold and her voice cracked all funny and low like walkin' on the pond when its freezin' up.

* * *

It was near three months since Lainey saw William, since the summer—July. It was October now and we had to go to school, so Lainey spent most of her time there. She didn't have as much responsibility for us kids because she had to do homework, go to cheerleadin' practice, and of course, hang out with all her friends. She did what she could do to stay out of the house and not have to look at Daddy's pitiful face, and Momma's sad face with more and more bruises. She spent a lot of time with Grandmom Sarah 'cause she couldn't deal with Momma and Daddy, *and* us kids, now even *during* the school year. She was real upset; she felt like we was robbin' her of her time with her friends and her own thoughts, how she truly felt inside.

And with Lainey, it seemed like boys was becomin' more popular, on her mind more and more.

Lainey sure liked hangin' out with her girlfriends at the Penn Supreme parlor, munchin' on cheese steaks, fries, and especially ice-cream. She *loved* mixin' Cheez-its with black cherry ice-cream. She'd pour some of them orange crackers right into her half-pint then smash 'em with the backside of her spoon; she liked the sweet-salty and the smooth-crunchy. Most of her friends was disgusted by the idea 'til they tried it on a dare. That day in October, Lainey said Jimmy and William came in with two other boys, the Deputy twins. She didn't even really know them, the Twins, 'cept they was very black and always shiny. She said the guys was all smilin' at each other like they had somethin' on everybody else.

"Lainey, what you still doin' here, girl? I know your momma is lookin' for you to come home and take care of them *kids*."

"Look, Jimmy, I ain't got time for them kids right now. They hers, not mine. I got stuff to do."

"Like what?" said William.

"Like bein' here so y'all could see us when you came in and so y'all can give us a ride to my house."

"We ain't goin' that a'way," said Jimmy.

This time, William gave Jimmy the elbow right in front of Lainey, like she couldn't see him do it.

"I guess we can give y'all a ride. Somebody's gonna have to sit on somebody's lap 'cause I got my other boys here with me,"

Jimmy said. Nobody else said nothin'. Lainey said she tried to hide what she was thinkin', but since William and her was the only ones who was even kinda familiar, she sat on his lap the whole ride to our house. We lived *way* out in the sticks, along some windy back roads around a coupla' blind turns, and when Jimmy took them corners too fast, Lainey fell more onto William 'til she was sittin' full center in his lap; she felt that heat again, but she still tried to think of *that* kind as new. They got out of the car at the roadside up the lane. When William got out to stretch his legs, Lainey grabbed *his* hand.

"Thanks for lettin' me use your lap."

"My pleasure. Anytime."

"Get my phone number from Jimmy if you want to call me. Just don't give him no more to drink. He drinks enough as it is. I trust y'all to get my girls straight home, right? It only takes about five minutes 'cross Sandtown Road and they gonna call me soon as they get in, *right?*"

William winked at Lainey and smiled when Jimmy peeled away down the dusty road.

* * *

When Lainey walked into the house, it was more quiet than usual. Everybody was sittin' down in the livin' room lookin' in the air, it seemed like, at somethin' invisible. Soon as Lainey came in, the two of us went right to the kitchen.

"Now what's goin' on?"

"Momma stabbed him."

"*What?*"

"I *said* 'Momma stabbed *Daddy.*'"

"Shush. Quiet down. When?"

"A little bit ago."

"Where?"

"On his side and on his neck. Right here and here. They started fussin' again in the livin' room about Daddy drinkin' up all the money, and she threw a bottle of liquor and it hit the TV and broke it right durin' *Mary Tyler Moore* and then they was fightin' in the kitchen and breakin' stuff and throwin' stuff aroun' and then he hit her right in her face and she went after him with the butcher knife. I think she was tryin' to kill him this time—for real!"

"That's it!" said Lainey. "I can't take no more of this shit. If he stays here then I'm leavin'. I'll go live with Grandmom Sarah or maybe I'll just run away."

"Then why you cryin' if you wanna leave?"

"I ain't cryin', I'm just mad that's all."

"I think I'm mad, too, but I'll sure be scared if you go."

* * *

William started callin' the very next day. First, Daddy answered the phone and William hung up. It rang again and Lainey raced for it, yellin', 'I got it!' from the top of the stairs flyin' in stockin' feet. She slipped down them last few steps right on her ass. It sure was a *sight!*

"Hello?"

"..."

"Speaking."

" . . . "

"I know," she said, smilin' from ear to ear.

They was on the phone all the time from then on, and for about two weeks or so, they met in secret. He would work the late, late shift at the Plant, the chicken factory over in Dover, pullin' out bird guts, then he'd meet her most of the time after cheerleadin'. He picked her up in his ol' truck and they drove to the beach or went somewhere to eat and talk. She asked him one time why he *never* said nothin' when she was sad. He told her he didn't ask 'cause she always seemed to get happy when they was together—he said he didn't want to make her sadder by talkin' about problems and stuff, so he didn't say nothin'. But then things started to come to the top when the two of them got close, and they didn't want to be away from one another. She *thought* they did a decent job keepin' secret from Momma and Daddy, but it was 1970, in a small, country town, and eventually, *everybody* knew everybody else's business. Sooner than later, word spread that Lainey been seen runnin' 'round town in some man's truck. William was twenty-two.

That day finally came 'round the middle of October. We was all gonna work on our Halloween costumes 'til Daddy saw William drop Lainey off at the end of the lane. She had reached all up in the window and they kissed a little too long, right smack on the lips. Daddy didn't say nothin' at first, but then later, when me and Lainey was cleanin' up the kitchen, he came in all puffed up.

"Elaine, who that boy you been hangin' 'round talkin' on the phone with all the time?"

"Nobody."

"Don't be playin' with me. Girl, get on in the livin' room."

"William, Jimmy's friend. Y'all met him before. We *just* friends."

"I don't know what kind of friends kiss like I saw up the lane. I *said* 'Finish up them dishes later and get on in the livin' room.' This here concerns Elaine and me. Now, get on!"

"What you spyin' on me for?"

"Cause I can, that's why. That boy is too old for you. Hell, *boy*? He's a full-grown man. What's a grown man want with a girl like you? I'll tell you what he wants. You *know* what he wants."

"Well he can *want* all he wants. We just friends."

"I best not see you 'round him again or hear tale about you and him ridin' 'round here all carefree. So you best tell him 'cause if I have to tell him..."

"I hear you! *Damn!*"

"Whatchu' just say?"

Lainey was all fired up, holdin' back her tongue. She said words like that all the time behind Daddy's back and under her breath. Never straight up to his face. She was quiet for a little bit and it seemed like she was gonna back down, then she cut loose.

"I'll see him if I want to! I don't care what you think or what you have to say after what you did to my mom! Why don't you take your drunk-ass on somewhere and leave us be?"

She looked Daddy right in his red eyes, stood strong-legged too, and waited for her words to come right back at her as a ashy, black hand up-side her face. She balled up her fist, closed her eyes and waited, but nothin' happened. When she opened her eyes, Daddy was sittin' on the couch starin' at the wall 'cause the TV was still broke. He got up and walked right past us and didn't even say a word before he slammed the door shut.

Lainey called Grandmom Sarah and told her Daddy left and Momma was still at the diner. She lied, too, said she was stayin' overnight at cousin Pammy's house before all this. Grandmom Sarah said she'd come over and sit with us kids 'til Daddy came back or Momma got home from work. Lainey couldn't wait. She ran upstairs, then after a little bit, she came back down in her baby blue church dress with her hair slicked and pulled back in a ponytail. She said Grandmom Sarah was comin' over and left us kids on our own. She met William up at the roadside end of the lane like usual. Lainey always said she wanted *some*body to take her *some*where, *anywhere*, as long it was away from Daddy, and she knew William and her *were* more than just friends, and maybe Daddy did have some reason to worry. But Daddy's ways made her want to be with William even more. She said she couldn't even believe what they was 'bout to do, but she sure knew she wanted to do it. She thought William would protect her and love her because he wanted *her*.

They did it right there in a field that very night. They picked twigs and leaves off each other and had to rub dirt out their clothes before Lainey got home. She was sure gonna have to face Momma and Daddy about what she said to Daddy, and what she was doin' and with who, and about leavin' us kids all alone. And William was sure gonna have to face Momma and Daddy, too, over Lainey. When she stepped up on the porch, she held on to the handle for a little bit before turnin' it. She said she was all wrapped up in William and never even wondered about the comin' July, a baby arrivin', her precious lil' Steven. When she walked in, she kicked an empty bottle across the floor, and lights came on, then on, then on.

*...boys make love and sex and chocolate cakes
that wind up twisted, on the streets,
with no icing. Mercy Me...*

INTERSECTION

ALONE

I mean, it didn't seem like such a big deal at the time. A lot of people around the world don't eat. It's not really a choice for most of them, like the kids in Africa or homeless people and stuff, but they go for *days* without a single bite. So, I figured it wouldn't be so bad sometimes to just, well…not eat. I don't know, I mean, I didn't really have major issues with my body like some of my friends did, like Lizzy and Cara for instance. They thought they needed to lose weight but they didn't and I was always like *What are you guys talkin' about? You look great!* But then they started skippin' lunch to drive around smokin' cigarettes, and then I started goin' with them but cigarettes made me want to throw up so I just chewed Big Red. Then I started gettin' *sooo* busy after school and hangin' out that I started missin' more and more meals and that plus the other equals me losin' weight, you see? Not really on purpose. It just kinda happened. After awhile, food just got boring. Like not interesting. Like *ooh, there's another dead piece of meat on my plate…ooh, steamed vegetables…rice…yum!* Anyway, it, like, kinda got away from me, that's all. I mean, I don't really have a problem because I didn't mean to get this way. I have a condition, *right?* All they have to do is hook me up to a machine to feed me, help me keep everything down 'til I get my strength back and then I can start eating again. Yeah, I'll keep goin' to therapy and stuff, but like I said, I don't want to be this way, so it won't be a problem, *right?* I'll just take a few weeks off from school, kids do it all the time as long as they get their work done and make-up their labs, you know, family vacations, funerals, rehab and stuff. You wait and see. Before you know it, I'll be puttin' on weight, I'll have my boobs back, my hair will stop fallin' out, maybe even start growin' in. I'll start havin' my period again, but, you *know*, it's been kinda nice not havin' it for awhile. I can hardly wait to get my teeth implants and my veneers. My smile will be even better than it was before. Lizzy and Cara will be *so* jealous.

MIRROR

She sat looking at the masking tape securing the black Hefty bag around her vanity mirror. She grabbed the top of the bag with her pale, bony index finger and thumb, then ran her other hand down the center to the bottom where she slowly began unwinding tape. The dresser's flat surface was covered with pig figurines: pink ceramic ones donning NASCAR uniforms, wood-carved ones in blue-painted overalls, glass ones dressed in tutus, and a family of small jade ones. She herded the pigs to the left side of the vanity with her left hand as she continued pulling tape with her right. The tape made a low, ripping sound. She scrunched her face into its center and hunched her shoulders, but she kept pulling. Once she tugged the tape half-way off of the bag, she stood up and began wrapping it around her forearm; her bone was visible through her translucent, blue-toned skin. She continued winding tape up to her elbow until the last piece tore from the bag, left a hole revealing a hint of reflection, and black plastic on the tape.

She stood in front of the mirror and breathed deeply; all twelve ribs pushed against her sheer white blouse. She grabbed both sides of the bag and began lifting it. She stopped when she got half-way up the mirror and then pulled the bag back down. She covered her face with her hand, felt her cheekbone, then sat down at the vanity and clicked on a small table lamp. For a few moments, she was motionless, and then she stood, grabbed the plastic bag, and pulled it up, over the full length of the mirror. There was an exposed section at the top; the rest of the mirror was covered in pictures of pigs: cut-outs from magazines, actual Polaroids, and close-ups of pig snouts and curly-tailed butts. She began pulling off large sections of pictures, revealing more and more mirror. She closed her eyes, felt around for the last pictures, ripped them off and opened her eyes at the same time.

She studied her face in the mirror, gently touched her reflection, traced its sharp edges, around the gaunt spaces of her eyes. She ran her fingers through her thin, dull-brown hair, and tossed the long strands entwined in them into the air. She watched the hairs float to the bare wood floor, then turned back to the mirror and tried to smile. Her thin, bluish lips barely parted to reveal rotting and missing teeth. She put her fingers into her mouth, felt the vacant spaces, and then stopped on a tooth, wiggled it between her fingers; it came out in her hand. She held it up to the mirror, examined it, rotating it in front of her face.

When she stood up, she wrapped her hand around her opposite wrist, completely covering her scar, and smiled; she repeated with the other hand, the slightly lower scar still visible. She then turned profile to the mirror and sucked in a breath. When she let out the breath, there was no visible sign of her stomach getting bigger or smaller. She lifted her blouse to reveal a sunken belly, a concave space comprised of thin skin pulled tightly across her shriveled breasts and between her ribs. She tried to wrap her hands around her waist, force them to meet each other by thumbs in front and pinkies at her back. After they almost touched, she simulated the width between her hands in the mirror. "Yes, almost there," she said into her reflection.

A car door slammed. She went to her bedroom window then peered between the blinds, squinting in the afternoon sun. She ran back to the vanity, grabbed the black plastic bag and pulled it over the mirror. She opened and closed the drawers, felt around inside of them, then held up her arm and began pulling the tightly wound tape. She placed the edge of the sticky side onto the bag and pressed. It fell off and then she pressed again, ground her thumb into the tape; this time it took. She furiously unwound tape around the bag and mirror, put on her sweatshirt, gathered her pig pictures into a pile, and then laid her head down on top of them as her doorknob turned.

DISTANCE

Relse's mom peeked her head around the door. She didn't know what to expect these days when she entered her daughter's room. Relse was sitting at her vanity with her head down on a pile of papers.

"Relse? Are you okay?"

Relse slowly lifted her head and looked at her mother.

"I'm fine." She stood up and her gray sweatshirt overtook her body, made everything but her head and sneakers disappear in cotton. "What are you guys doing back so early? I thought you were going to the meeting after Dad picked you up?"

"Well, the meeting's not until six, so I decided to come home and drop some things off, and well, of course, to see *you*. I was hoping, *maybe*, you'd come with me?"

Loretta felt the hopelessness of her words as they left her mouth. She knew Relse had not changed her mind, but she couldn't imagine herself, alone, in front of a roomful of strangers, on the verge of crying.

"No thanks. I think I'm gonna stay here and watch some TV. I *am* feelin' a little tired."

"Are you sure everything's okay, Honey? I could call Dr. Montgomery?"

"*No, Mom*. I told you, no more doctors. I hate them pokin' at me, touchin' me all the time. *I hate* the way it makes me *feel*."

"But…"

"I told you what I would do if you made me go. No more… *please?*"

Loretta watched her daughter's face contort and tears trickle. She didn't like seeing Relse upset. She knew that, no matter how Relse was feeling, her insistence would make Relse feel even worse, maybe for days. Loretta stepped further into the room and reached for her daughter. Relse moved a little closer and extended her bony arm. They held hands, from a distance.

CHANNEL-SURFING

"So, did you tell her she *has* to see a doctor again? yelled Richard, roaming channels via his forty-two inch, plasma TV.

"Of course I *told* her she has to see a doctor. I even mentioned calling Dr. Montgomery," said Loretta from the kitchen.

"And?"

"And she said what she's been saying for the past three months."

"That she'd try it again?"

"Right. I just didn't want to push her, not today."

"Why not?"

"I don't know. Just not today."

Loretta came into the Media room and then sat in the chair next to Richard. He would not look at her but kept channel-surfing. He didn't want to see his wife's face as it had taken on a hyper-fakeness, an almost carved expression of contentment. He hated watching her lie about how okay she was with their daughter's condition; but, what he really feared was seeing his own face, of recognizing himself in his wife's denial.

"So, are you still going to the meeting?"

"I *have* to go," said Loretta flipping through a magazine.

"You don't *have* to go."

"Of course I have to go. I *finally* have to go."

Richard did not respond. He squirmed in his chair. The word 'finally' had struck him; it was the first time he heard her say it or any version: the end, death, crossing over. He pressed the remote control buttons harder.

"Well, then, I guess I'm gonna go. She said she was going to watch some TV and rest for a bit. *Please* check in on her."

Loretta walked to Richard and kissed him on the cheek. He stopped channel-surfing but refused to look.

"I will."

PUKING

She reached into the medicine cabinet, pulled out a yellow hair binder, and then turned on the hot water in the shower. She grabbed for loose strands of hair by her ears and pulled them back with her left hand. She wrapped the binder around and let go, bringing a few more strands of hair in her hand. She pulled the small, red wastebasket from the corner then grabbed the rug underneath it, placed the rug in front of the toilet. Her knees slammed down hard and she wobbled side to side, held the silver trash can lid for balance. She lifted the toilet lid and seat, examined the bowl, then rubbed her stomach, stuck all four fingers down her throat as her thumb massaged her jaw. Tears fell down her face as she began to dry heave, and then, threw up a clear liquid into the bowl. She flushed the toilet then jammed her thumb into her mouth as well. Loudly retching, she flushed the toilet again, then quickly again, and wiped her mouth with the backside of her hand. She got up slowly from the floor sliding the rug, with her foot, back into the corner. After she placed the wastebasket, she stood in front of the medicine-cabinet and touched where the mirror should be. She stuck out her tongue, placed a dab of toothpaste on the tip, grabbed her toothbrush off the back edge of the sink, and then began furiously brushing her tongue.

BREATH

"Relse, Honey, I'm taking off. Are you sure there isn't anything I can get for you? Some juice, maybe?"

"No, Mom, I'm *okay*. I'll get something in a little bit, I promise."

Loretta pressed her ear to the door and listened, tried to distinguish any unusual sounds over the running water.

"Okay, I told your father to check in on you. Maybe you can go downstairs and watch TV with *him*?"

"Maybe."

"Well...okay then, I'm leaving. I'll see you later. Are you *sure...*"

"Yes, Mom, I'm sure I don't wanna go."

"Okay, then. I love you."

"Me too."

"Bye."

Loretta walked away from the door towards the stairs. She stopped for a moment at the edge of the stairwell and then went back to the bathroom door. As she pressed her ear against the door, she held her breath to not make any noise. After a few seconds, she headed back to the stairs. During her descent, she realized that she was still holding her breath, then she let go.

CONFRONTATION

Richard opened the refrigerator and stuck his head inside. He began pulling out items and placing them on the counter: fried pork chops   mashed potatoes   meatloaf   mac & cheese string beans   fried chicken   something in a takeout container   something else in a takeout container   orange cheese   lettuce   ketchup   barbecue sauce   mustard. He closed the refrigerator door then opened it, put back the mustard. He stood with his hands on the counter looking at the food, then, he opened the refrigerator and—item by item—placed it all back, watched his tears drop to then run down the sides of plastic-wrapped pieces of meat.

CONFESSION

Good afternoon, everyone. Well, um, my name is Loretta, and I'm here because I'm at my wits' end with my daughter, Relse. She was the sweetest, cutest little girl you have *ever* seen, I mean, *really*. She had the smoothest ivory skin, and the smallest, most precious little brown curls on top of her head. She didn't cry a lot either, always smiling. When she was born, and I finally had my little girl, I thought my life was perfect. I even remember saying to myself, *Now, I can be truly happy.* I just looked forward to watching her grow up, become the vibrant young woman that I had been, ready to take on the world, take on anything. I mean, she played tennis, she was a cheerleader, and she never got anything less than an 'A,'...*never.* She was one of the most popular girls in her class every year, and this year she met who I thought was the perfect boy for her: tall, smart, from a nice family, good manners, and *great* hair. You know what I mean?

The kind of boy you want at your door calling on your daughter. It was all so perfect, and then, well, I don't know what happened. One day I looked up, saw this girl dressed in baggy clothes, a baseball cap, empty eyes. My husband said 'I think she's doing drugs'. I knew that my Relse would never get hooked on drugs, especially something that would make her look like *that!* I bet it was those horrible girls she started hanging out with, those fast girls with the even *faster* bodies. I mean, they look like full-grown women! I should've noticed she wasn't just missing meals, but *skipping* meals all together. I should've seen something sooner. *I'm* her mother. She came from *my* body. Now, frankly, I don't even like going into her room. There's this heaviness, a sour, almost wet odor that *only* makes me think of my little girl dying. She wouldn't get rid of her vanity, so her therapist told her to cover the mirror. It's taped over with a black Hefty bag. I don't like it. No, I really don't. I think she *should* see herself. See what she's doing to her body, what she's doing to her family—to ME! Can any of you explain it? Can anybody in this room tell me why my little girl won't eat? Why she wants to die?

WORKOUT

Relse reached under her bed, pulled out an orange yoga mat, then unrolled it in the space between her vanity and bed. She lay down on her back and stared at the ceiling. Tired, but determined to stay on her workout schedule, she took some deep breaths and closed her eyes. It came rushing back to her. *I'm at the dinner table and there's a big green and red shiny salad in a clear bowl. My mom and dad aren't talking as usual and there's something still cooking in the oven. My mom gets up and walks to the kitchen. I'm looking at her over my father's head. He's looking down at his empty plate. My mom takes off aluminum foil from a large pan; there's a humongous roast. The steam and smells rise from the pan and my dad looks up. He catches my eyes and manages a little smile; then he looks back down at his plate. My mom puts the large piece of meat on a white platter, brings it over to the table, then sets it in the middle next to the sorry salad and mashed potatoes. She picks up the knife and serving fork and starts carving. When the knife moves down into the meat, blood oozes onto the plate until a slice is cut. The pink and red startle me and I look at my dad's sweaty forehead. She pierces a piece of the roast and holds it out to him, dripping blood on the white table cloth, and then his plate, before she drops it on the spot he's been staring at all night.*

She reaches out for my plate and I give it to her. She places a piece of the roast on it and I try to smile. We pass the potatoes and the salad. I get up to get the bread from the counter, and when I do, I look back at them. I hope they are looking at each other, but they're both sawing away at their meat. There's only the clinking of their knives against the plates. "Bread?" They both look relieved that I broke the silence and that they didn't have to do it. I hand a piece to each of them at the same time. I grab one for myself, but instead of eating it, I use it to sop up all the blood rushing towards my potatoes.

Relse opened her eyes and crossed her hands behind her head. She bent her knees, planted her feet on the floor, took another deep breath, and then started doing sit-ups.

"One...two......three.........four..........."

DISCOVERY

Richard pressed the mute button, jutted his head into the air, cocked his ear, and listened for noise from upstairs. He turned off the TV and then went to the kitchen. He reached for Relse's favorite orange glass, opened the refrigerator, and took out a pitcher of juice. He grabbed saltines from the cupboard and placed three of them on a saucer, stopping as the thought of this being too much food for his daughter made him shiver. He put back two of the crackers and was then confronted by the lone white cracker on the orange saucer. He knew that this could be the only thing she had eaten all day. Then, he thought about his sadness, of her refusal of the cracker, how it would make him feel; he put the solitary saltine back into the box, blew crumbs off of the saucer, and then poured the juice.

"Relse? Relse, Baby, I brought you some orange juice!" said Richard knocking on the door. He knocked a little louder. "Relse? Are you awake? Relse?"

Richard placed his hand on the doorknob and slowly turned. He opened the door and steadied his eyes on his daughter lying on the mat. The glass crashed to the wood, and orange shards and juice sprayed across the floor. He went to her, knelt by her side, gently placed his head on her chest and listened. He tried hard to see the vibrant girl of just two years ago, but the protruding bones would not allow it. He raised his head, cupped his hands around her face, and then tightly closed his eyes.

DRIVE

She did feel better after the meeting. She didn't talk to anybody—rushed out—but the fact that she had said anything at all was a huge step. Driving, she searched her brain for what she would say to her daughter once she got home. Was there anything *to* say? Was there only the waiting left? A sense of relief came over her, quickly followed by a wave of guilt. She turned up the radio to drown the sound of her voice inside her head. The ride seemed surprisingly short, and as she pulled into her driveway behind the ambulance, she cut her lights…felt herself steadying herself.

PARAMEDIC

He put on his latex gloves and checked her body for vital signs: breathing, pulse, eye movement. He was afraid to start CPR, as compressions would surely crack more than the usual few ribs, increasing the chances of puncturing a lung. He tilted her head then began breathing slowly into her mouth. His partner pulled the sobbing father away and consoled him. He pressed on her chest and studied her face, touched her bony ribcage, stunned by her torso's concavity. He thought to himself that the girl hadn't eaten anything substantial in awhile. Who would let their daughter waste away like this? Why wasn't she in a hospital? What about those scars? When her eyes slowly opened, he called over to his partner and the girl's father. His partner hooked the IV bag to the post then slid the needle into her emaciated arm. He fastened the belts around her body, and then they hoisted the gurney. The girl's father placed his hand on her shoulder as the EMTs wheeled her through the door to the edge of the stairwell.

"Honey," the man said to the woman standing at the foot of the stairs.

They stopped the gurney and let her father step past and down. The EMT looked at his partner and thought about the questions again, this time searching the mother's face for answers.

INTERSECTION

The evening traffic parted. The ambulance's blue and red lights flashed as they drove closely behind it. Neither of them said anything; spoke a word about their daughter. They fumbled for each others' hand—grasped—squeezed. At the red light, moving cautiously through the intersection, they looked at each others' face.

SEEING

She could feel them touching her: tapping on her feet, lifting her arms, pulling her eyelids up. It was the hospital room smell that made her not want to open her eyes. She sensed the tubes and wires connected to her body. The pumping sound, like shallow breathing, informed her that she was not living by herself, on her own. The people in the room talked as if she couldn't hear them, but she identified the four voices: her mother, father, therapist, and doctor. When she slowly opened her eyes, she noticed her parents in the corner, arms wrapped tightly around each other, and her therapist in a chair, his brown hand furiously writing in a notebook. When her doctor called them over, a faint, toothless smile was all she could muster.

...I ain't got none for you. Mercy Me. I ain't got none for you...

LAUNDRY NIGHT

"So you're sayin' you can't baby-sit tonight?"

" . . . "

"You know this is my laundry night and I don't like takin' 'Retha with me."

" . . . "

" 'Cause she told me she hates it that's why. You know she gets antsy and wants to run all around gettin' into stuff and you know I use my laundry time to relax and think."

" . . . "

"I know I took her before, only when *you* backed out of watchin' her."

" . . . "

"Well you know what, I guess it don't really matter anyway. It's not like it's the first time and I'm sure it won't be the last."

" . . . "

"Yeah, bye *asshole*."

Felicia slammed the phone down and screamed. She needed this night, the third Saturday of the month, to do the laundry. Doing it weekly seemed too time-consuming since she didn't have her own washer and dryer to use. It would also mean finding someone to watch 'Retha and paying the sitter money she didn't have or could use for laundry. Felicia enjoyed the emptiness on Saturday nights as few people went to this particular Laundromat, Camden Coin-Operated; it wasn't in the best shape, and it was directly across from Ash & Sons Funeral Home. She liked the strange quiet: the soft shake of wash cycles, the rinse cycles almost like rain, and the dryers' gentle vibrations. There is also something about the smell of detergents and fabric softeners that relaxed her, like fresh April showers and new teddy bears. This night was the worst to be sitter-less, March 16th, 1975, her 25th birthday, and the anniversary of her twin sister's death in 1970. Felicia was normally wound tight, but each year as this day approached, the anxiety, depression, and guilt surrounding her sister's death would gradually overwhelm her.

"'Retha, go get your laundry basket and let's get ready to go. Your sorry-ass daddy ain't comin'."

'Retha looked at her mother and tugged the edges of her yellow knit dress. Her skin was smooth, medium-brown with buttery undertones, and her black hair rose roundly from her head in a button mushroom afro.

"*Well?* Go get your *basket.*" Felicia looked through her daughter.

"But what about *my* present?"

"Never mind that, just go get your damn basket and come on, 'Retha. *Now!*"

'Retha turned and headed down the long hallway in their project apartment. The walls were dingy white, and the carpet: matted shag in three shades of mustard. 'Retha was taking too long, so Felicia crept to 'Retha's bedroom and then peeked around the door. The room was sparse. There was a little bed and an adult-sized dresser with a small, oval, princess mirror embossed in fancy pewter. 'Retha pulled open her closet by the plastic handle then slid out her full laundry basket. She paused for a moment and then opened the other sliding door. Inside were crates of her aunt's old records, all 45s, stacked to the ceiling, and a microphone with a long, black cable winding on the floor. She ran her little fingers across the crates and records, picked up the microphone, held it to her mouth, put her left hand on her hip, and then, with gusto beyond her five years, began furiously mouthing words.

"'Retha! Come on here now! I ain't got all damn night. Get your basket and let's *go!*"

'Retha watched her mother turn then walk away. She closed her closet door and picked up the almost too big basket, peeking around the corner as she walked the hall.

"I don't wanna go wash no clothes."

"And I don't want you to go neither, but I guess we can't always get what we want. Now come on here." Felicia walked out of the apartment and let the door close, almost knocking over 'Retha and her basket. 'Retha side-stepped the door like a Temptation. It locked automatically.

* * *

Felicia hoped that the Coin-Op would be empty at nine o'clock on a Saturday night. There are only a few machines, and at least one of them is usually out of order. There were two other cars in the lot when she backed her Gremlin up to the front of the building. She got out of her car and then slammed the door as the hatchback popped open. 'Retha sat motionless in the front seat.

"'Retha, get out and get your basket and bring the bleach too."

Felicia walked up to the Coin-Op and the girl outside of the door, smoking a cigarette, grabbed the handle and pulled the door wide. Felicia nodded quickly, walked in, and then sat down her basket in a chair facing the parking lot. She wiped the steamy window with a t-shirt and peered out. 'Retha got out of the car, closed the door, pulled her basket out of the hatchback, and then placed it on the ground. She hopped up to the back, rolled the bleach towards her and scurried backwards out to her basket. She stood on the mound of clothes and reached up to close the pea-green hatch. She buried the bleach bottle under her dirty laundry, lifted the basket, and then headed to the door. The girl smoking the cigarette had gone inside.

* * *

Felicia was in her favorite corner of the Coin-Op, the one where the TV and vending machine are, but farthest from the bathroom, as it was also frequently out of order. The woman who opened the door was aggressively chewing gum and styling her dusty-brown hair in the glass dryer door, her reflection swirling with underwear and t-shirts. The owner of the other car sat in the seat next to the bathroom reading a *Jet* magazine with Diana Ross and Billy Dee Williams on the cover. She read over her eyeglasses and squinted, moved the magazine closer then farther away. Gray hairs peeked from under her red scarf and she openly picked her nose. 'Retha sat in a green plastic lawn chair next to the row of off-white Maytag washers, under the large window facing the funeral home. She watched her mother sort women's panties, bras, and slacks into separate washing machines, sprinkle in laundry detergent, and then close the lids. She took 'Retha's basket and dumped all of the clothes into one washer; she scooped some detergent with her hand then threw it in.

Felicia moved inside the Coin-Op as if on stage. She lifted machine lids and tossed clothes from washer to dryer, shuffling quarters in her pockets, hands, and through machine slots. 'Retha sat in the chair eating candy, the only thing that her mom did for her at the Coin-Op: candy bars, hard candy, licorice, chews, anything and everything to keep her quiet, in the chair, and out of the way. The TV had only one dial, and though it was anchored to the wall, high in the corner, the reception was bad. Felicia stood on a chair and turned the TV dial—channel after channel of snowy lines and continuously running horizontal pictures. She tried adjusting the hold with the small white button in back of the TV.

"'Retha, what's it doin'? Is it a good picture yet?"

"Nope."

"What about now?"

"Nope. It don't even work."

"Shit." Felicia stepped off of the chair. She looked at 'Retha sitting with her candy and then towards the machines spinning their clothes. "*Now* what am I supposed to do?"

'Retha looked at her mom, shrugged her shoulders, crammed piece after piece of gum into her mouth, and then began chewing. Felicia turned off the TV and stared into its blankness.

* * *

The man looked dirty. His white skin was eerily grayed and he ushered his wiry frame to the center folding table. His scruffy beard seemed the perfect place for varmints, and his short, reddish-blonde hair was in patches, as if scratched with the end of a spoon for hidden creatures below his scalp. His holey "I'm with stupid" t-shirt was stained with something red, his dirty tan khakis reeked of piss, and his Converse had no shoestrings. He wore a pair of large white headphones not plugged into anything, a long black cord, trailing. He pulled out a handful of quarters then placed it in a mound in the center of the table. He picked up a quarter, examined it, and then put it back into the pile. He picked up another quarter and did the same thing. He took off his shoes, socks, examined his grungy socks, and then began searching for a dryer instead of a washer. He put the socks in the dryer, took them out, put them on, and slid his feet into his Chuck Taylors.

While folding, Felicia watched the man's peculiar behavior, and then looked at 'Retha who was involved with an apple-green strand of taffy stretched from her tightly-clenched teeth to the length of her arm. The man walked to the vending machine and ran his hand over his reflection in the glass. 'Retha gently kicked his headphone cord as she continued her match with the candy. He turned back to his mound of quarters. She kicked his leg. When he looked at her, she smiled and offered him a Mary Jane.

"'Retha, what I tell you about talkin' to strangers, girl? You—, get the hell away from her!"

The man turned red under his grayness. He ran to the table, scooped up his quarters, then fled out the door, tripping over his cord as he stumbled through the parking lot.

"Huh? she said, walking towards 'Retha. "What did I tell you?"

'Retha's eyes were wide and the corners of her mouth had remnants of chocolate. She didn't speak, but kept chewing.

"If I catch you again, I'm taking all the candy away, you hear me? ALL OF THE CANDY!"

She nodded and continued chewing. When her mom left her side, she climbed into the chair and watched the man run down the road, past the funeral home. The woman with the *Jet* magazine drank steadily from a large bottle of Tab, and the brown-haired woman folded white clothes and placed them in a black trash bag on the floor. The woman stood up and headed to the bathroom with her magazine. Shortly, a scream along with a stream of water erupted from behind the door. The brown-haired woman ran to the bathroom then pulled open the door, revealing the woman—skirt to ankles—on the floor clenching the *Jet* magazine, in water running non-stop from the faucet. Felicia peered from behind the door and offered a hand to the woman who continued screaming. Seconds later, she turned back to her laundry; 'Retha was not in her chair, but instead, a pile of candy wrappers.

* * *

Felicia paced outside the Coin-Op with the woman who had fallen in the bathroom. Fortunately, the woman had clean, dry clothes, and could immediately launder her soiled ones. The cops arrived half an hour later: two white guys with mustaches. The girl was pulling out of the driveway in her station wagon when they arrived. Felicia cried on the woman's shoulder as the cops approached.

"Felicia Jones?"

"Yes?"

"We came as soon as we could. Have you checked around the premises for your daughter? Out back? In the woods?" The cops scribbled in their junior notebooks.

"Of course I fuckin' checked around. We checked *everywhere*. She's not here! She's gone! *Please* help me find her!" Felicia was in their faces now, tears streaming, eyes bulging and bloodshot.

"I know this is a difficult time Ms. Jones, but try to remain calm, we *are* here to help. How long has she been missing?"

"Thirty...forty minutes by now. I don't know...I'm not sure. I was doing laundry, then the water and the screaming, and when I turned around, she was..."

The cops continued writing while glancing at each over their pads.

"Were there any strangers around?"

"There was this homeless-lookin' white guy wearing headphones and dirty socks who was here and I chased him away. Do you think he took my little girl? You think he hurt my baby?"

"We don't know Ms. Jones. We'll check around back to see if there's a clue somewhere. Is there anybody else she could've left with, any place she could've tried to get to? Where's her daddy?"

Felicia thought about where he was: in the delivery room with his girlfriend, having a new baby, on *my* birthday, on his *daughter's* birthday. She fell into the woman's arms and cried.

"He couldn't take her tonight."

* * *

An hour passed. The owner of the Laundromat, a chubby, small-headed black man with large shaded glasses, showed up in a rust-colored polyester suit. He paced the street. The woman, Miss Louise Freed, kissed Felicia on the cheek then walked to her car. She slowly drove away waving back at the scene. Felicia sat in the rear of her open Gremlin, facing the Coin-Op, barely able to hear the cops talk about increasing the scope of the search, calling in more help, phoning the newspapers and maybe even the FBI. She reached into her pocket and pulled out a tissue. A caramel fell to the ground. She dried her eyes, blew her nose, and then bent for the candy; when she rose, she unwrapped it then placed it into her mouth. She watched the Coin-Op owner walk up and down the streets under the mid-March moon. She moved towards him, working the caramel from her teeth with her tongue.

"Why didn't you fix the bathroom and those other machines? This could be a nice place if you…if you had fixed the bathroom, if I didn't have to help Miss Louise off her ass, then my…my…." She erupted into tears again.

Headlights appeared from around the dark corner, followed by a long, white hearse that, instead of pulling into Ash & Sons Funeral home across the street, stopped in the road at the edge of the Coin-Op's parking lot. The cops walked towards the hearse; Felicia and Mr. Oscar (the Coin-Op's owner) followed. The tinted window lowered, and an old, fair-skinned white man with graying reddish-brown hair nodded politely. He put his arm out the window and patted the door like a puppy.

"When I was drivin' this here baby back to Pennsylvania, I heard this sweet, beautiful voice, seemed like it was comin' from the radio, but when I turned the radio down, the voice got louder and sweeter. I pulled over and looked in back under the casket cover and there she was. She wouldn't tell me her name and all she wanted was candy, so I just turned this here baby around and started callin' her 'Candy.' She said her mom was doin' laundry and that it's her birthday."

'Retha emerged from the other side of the hearse chewing something red, carrying a clear plastic bag full of candy, trailing a black cord attached to large white headphones that swallowed up her head. She walked to her mother holding out the bag of candy. Felicia pulled off the headphones and dropped them. She looked at 'Retha, touched and studied her face, kissed it and the sweet redness that lingered at the edges of her mouth. She grabbed her daughter's hand, reached her other hand deep into the bag, and then pulled out a handful of candy. As they walked towards the Laundromat, Felicia tossed the candy back over her shoulder, high into the air. She giggled as she opened the door for 'Retha; 'Retha smiled and strolled by. Felicia had forgotten how much 'Retha favored her as a little girl, how much 'Retha reminded Felicia of her twin sister, then: young, alive, a part of her. They gathered clothes and laundry supplies into their baskets and went to the car. Mr. Oscar, the cops, and Mr. Ash-the hearse driver, were still outside talking. Felicia popped the hatchback, placed her basket inside, and then helped 'Retha place hers in as well. They both reached for the trunk, and, half-way down, closed it together. When 'Retha spotted the pink box with a yellow ribbon on the passenger's seat, Felicia's hands crossed, instinctively, over her own heart.

...Chicken pox and pots of chicken, Colonel says 'They're finger lickin'!' but what about those who...

DREAD

The day after Family Night, Kevin, sitting crossed-legged in the center of the backyard where he used to play trucks, began making mud, twisting his short, perfectly golden hair into rope, slathering and caking mud into his blonde legacy. When his mother saw this, she had been cutting potatoes in the sink, looking out the window. She screamed a terrible scream, slipped, and accidentally cut off her left thumb. Kevin, muddy face and hair, looked up towards the window at his mother's horrified face, blood running down the glass as she pressed the pane. That was six years ago, in the summer of 1999, when he was thirteen. Now, at nineteen, his less-than-golden, brown dreadlocks hang just above his bellybutton. He hasn't seen his parents since just before his eighteenth birthday; he severed contact except for their voices on his answering machine. He is an only child. He hates to admit it, but during screening his calls, every time he listens to his messages, he hopes the one from them will be what he's wanted all along—the apology he has awaited since that day before he changed his hair and his life.

* * *

Stan's Pawn World closed early on Saturday nights: 10 P.M.; it used to be midnight, but Saturdays had proven to be the nights people were likely to come in drunk and rowdy, try to hock stolen merchandise, and steal. Kevin finished dusting the last of the TVs, and then placed the red feather duster on the hook behind the counter. He took off his headphones and went to the door at exactly ten o'clock. He turned the interior lock then began pulling down the gate from overhead, when a woman with dark brown hair and bulging eyes, dressed in a pink dress, emerged carrying an armful of electronic gadgets and desperation on her face and in her body. He looked into the woman's eyes and shook his head, sorrowfully, side to side.

"We're closed."

"Pleeaaase!"

"I'm sorry but I already started the Z-report and I can't ring up anything even if I wanted to. Sorry."

He closed the gate and turned off the light. He could sense her, still, standing there. He finished up and headed home, periodically shaking the image of the woman out of his mind.

* * *

Kevin's phone was ringing as he unlocked his door. He ran in, stood by the answering machine, and waited as he kicked off his sandals into the living room, one striking the TV.

"Hi, Kev-y! It's Mom. Are you there? If you are, please pick up... Please Kev-y, we're your family, your only family. Won't you just talk to us? Okay, then, maybe you're not home. I'll call again soon. Your father misses you too. Well, I love you. Okay, then, bye-bye."

Kevin wiped his forehead with one of his long, roped dreads and then listened to the rest of his messages—ten of them, all from his mother. Since his eighteenth birthday, when he denied his parents celebrating his official entry into adulthood, she had begun to call him more frequently—first a couple of calls a week, then a call every other day, then everyday, then multiple calls per day—but none ever with the apology, and in the past ten months, no calls from his father. He listened to and then erased all of the messages. It was 11:30. He pulled open the fridge and grabbed a beer from the case his neighbor bought for him every week. He also took out one of the white, Styrofoam carry-out containers, and a pack of shredded, bright-orange cheese. He opened the container, briefly reacted to the smell by slightly pulling away, and dumped the remainder of the cheese on top. He slid the entire concoction onto a paper plate, then into the microwave. He opened the cupboard above the microwave which was filled front to back, top to bottom, with chicken noodle soup cans donning red and white labels. He strategically pulled a can from the right side of the stack, untwisted its bottom, and then pulled out a clear plastic bag. He took out a lighter, an orange glass pipe, and a smaller bagful of weed. He pinched off some of the bud and packed it in the bowl, placed the pipe to his lips, then struck the lighter to flame. He breathed in deeper than he had expected and began choking out the smoke. Tears fell and he let them flow. He struck the lighter once more and inhaled. The microwave beeped and the phone rang simultaneously: the machine picked up.

"Hi, Kev-y, it's Mom, are you there?"

He did not exhale.

* * *

Sunday morning. The phone rang the first time at 7:15 A.M. (when his mom came home, like clock-work, from her morning run.) It rang again at 8:15 over Frosted Flakes, and at 8:45 on his way out the door to work. When he arrived, per Stan's instructions, he picked up loose cups and cigarette packs and then crammed them into the overflowing trash can outside. Sunday mornings were usually quiet; he looked forward to listening to music and reading music mags with few interruptions.

Kevin had a cell phone, but he hadn't given his parents the number. His mother had pleaded for it in several messages left on his machine. *'Kev-y, I could call you on your cell phone if you give me your number.'* Once, she left the same message all week: *'Kev-y, this is your mom, you can call me on my cell phone at 555-5372 or I can call you on your cell phone. Let me know what your number is and we can talk. Okay? Hope to hear from you soon. I love you, bye.'* It had taken him awhile to realize how his mom knew for sure that he had a cell phone, until last week at dinner with his childhood friend, Celeste. She's the pastor's daughter of the church he went to as a kid, the one his parents still attend. She had told Kevin that she worries about him working at Stan's because of shady people who deal in 'resold objects.' He had given her the number to make her feel better. The fact must've slipped out to his mother during the after-service mingling. Hopefully, Celeste hadn't succumbed and given his mother the number.

Kevin continued with his specific opening procedures: immediately locking the door after he was inside, using only the floor safety-lights until he got to the cash register, flicking the overhead lights when he was securely at the main counter, checking the back, powering up the rest of the store, and lastly, keying into the register. Kevin bent down, pulled aside the black and yellow rubberized Stan's Pawn World mat, and then lifted a panel of flooring via a small crack in the floor. The safe was underneath. He quickly rotated the combination

dial, pulled open the small door, and scooped out the deposit
bag. He counted the cash: five-hundred dollars, then placed it
in the register. He unlocked the front door; there was no line
outside. He tied back his dreadlocks with a bandana then put
on his headphones. He grabbed the feather duster and began
bopping around, lightly dusting the components. The phone
at Stan's barely rang on Sundays except for the occasional, 'Are
you open?' or 'When do you close?' When it rang, it took him
a moment to distinguish it over the R & B mix blaring in his
ears.

"Thank you for calling Stan's Pawn World. This is Kevin, how
can I help you?"

There was momentary silence and then his mother's voice.

"Hi, Kev-y, Honey. It's Mom. I…"

"Didn't Celeste tell you not to call me at work?"

"I know, Sweetie, but I…"

"You what?"

"I…I…"

"Goodbye, Mother."

Kevin hung up and then paced behind the counter while
swatting the phone with the duster. He grabbed a magazine
from under the counter and flipped through it, not stopping
long enough on one page to actually read anything, turning
pages more like a fan than for information. He closed the
magazine then tossed it to the floor. The phone rang as he put
on his headphones.

"Thank you for calling Stan's Pawn World. This is Kevin, how can I help you?"

"Kev-y, we must have lost our connection or something. Won't you please come over for dinner tonight or just drop by?"

"Mother, don't call here again. This is where I work."

"But you won't answer at home or call back; you return all of our cards and letters, and you still haven't given me your cell. How long is this going to go on?"

"As long as it takes."

"Kev-y, you know that we love you but..."

"Then, don't call me! Goodbye!"

Kevin slammed down the receiver then put on his headphones. A few people were window shopping TVs, but continued on by. He grabbed the duster and the phone rang. He looked at it, but let it keep ringing. This happened nonstop for the next hour. When he did pick up the phone, he abandoned his usual 'Thank you for calling Stan's...' for 'Stan's.' He immediately hung up when he heard his mother's voice. This occurred at least twice during the next few hours. He eventually grew more aggravated and turned off the ringer to let the answering machine pick up the calls.

* * *

His cell phone rang the entire ride home. He figured Celeste must have given in to his mother's whining, so he dared not answer it. At one point, he was tempted to throw it out the window. He heard his home phone ringing and then his machine pick up as he approached his apartment door. He entered to his mother's sighs and near-tears through his answering machine; it was blinking a red '24,' one message away from full.

"Please, please call me back, Kev-y, day or night. I love you and miss you and so does your father. We're never going to give up on you even if you've given up on us. Never. You are our only child and our future whether you want to be or not. Call me, okay? I love you so much, Kev-y. Bye."

The answering machine blinked full.

* * *

Laying on the floor, Kevin stared up at the ceiling and puffed a joint; in the smoke, his dreadlocks snaked away from his head along the matted carpet. Sundays had been special when he was growing up. His mother would cook large dinners for just the three of them: turkey and all of the fixins. There had been recent moments when he found himself thinking about the food, especially when he was munching through a bag of corn chips or devouring take-out and another tasteless snack cake. The smell of the all-day cooking had heightened his senses, and while his mother cooked, he and his father would watch TV or roam around and through the kitchen in search of dinner samples. He missed the warmth in the air, the security of his father's arms, and his mother's smile. His stomach grumbled and he rolled over to his belly, rubbed out the joint on the coffee table leg. His phone continued ringing, but with the answering machine being full, it would not pick up. He thought about scrounging something to eat; instead, he pulled his locks over his face, his knees towards his chest, and opted for a post-high nap.

He woke up to his stomach rumbling and the phone ringing. He thought he smelled his mother's turkey, but passed it off as munchies, wishful-thinking. As he got up off of the floor, the aroma seemed to grow stronger. The phone continued to ring. He rubbed his belly with both hands and headed towards the kitchen. There was a knock at the door, and as he approached it, phone still ringing, he opened it to the sight of his mother, cell phone to ear, holding Tupperware and a foil-wrapped plate of Sunday dinner, slightly steaming.

* * *

Kevin had begun to outgrow the Sunday dinner ritual. It was 1999, the summer heading into eighth grade. He and Tyrone had met at tennis camp in the beginning of summer, and he was thrilled that they would be attending the same school in the fall. Tyrone's family was in the process of moving from Oakland, California, to the elite development outside of Rehoboth Beach. His father was heading a new treatment center in Milton, and his family would be the first Black family in the exclusive community. That they lucked into meeting each other at a tennis camp in Las Vegas was kismet. They were inseparable at camp as they were evenly-matched tennis players; after Tyrone's family settled in toward the latter part of July, he and Kevin were attached at the hip, on and off of the tennis court. Kevin liked Ty's music, the way he talked, his clothes, and his family. On the court, he admired Ty's complete game and style, especially the way his long, black dreadlocks flew out from and around his head when he hit the ball. His own short, impeccably cut blonde hair stayed close to his head; his mother would never let it grow past his ears. They spent more and more time together: at Ty's, on the beach, on the courts, everywhere except Kevin's. He had begun to miss a few dinners, preferring to eat on the boardwalk, grabbing a slice of pizza somewhere with Ty. This particular Sunday he wanted to hang out with Ty, but it was Family Night and his mother would be cooking in the kitchen all day. An idea popped into his head while watching his father watch football.

"Hey, Dad, can Ty come over for dinner tonight?"

Kevin's dad squirmed a little in his recliner.

"Well, Kev, I don't know. It *is* Family Night and you know how your mother likes it to be just the three of us. Tradition and all of that good stuff."

Kevin dropped his head and sighed.

"*Please*, just this one time?"

"I don't think so Kev. Sorry."

Kevin got up from the couch then headed into the kitchen. His mom was busy stirring gravy and swirling green beans with tongs.

"Hey, Kev-y. Dinner is gonna be extra special tonight. I'm making something new just for you!"

Kevin leaned against the fridge. "What is it?"

"A surprise. Just wait, you'll love it!"

"Why?"

"Well, Sweetheart, it seems like I rarely get to see you anymore. I mean, with you spending so much time with Tyrone."

"He likes to be called 'Ty.'"

"Well, since he's moved here it's like I lost my baby a little bit that's all. So, I wanted to do something unique just for you."

Kevin tried to smile. "Mom, can Ty come over for dinner tonight?"

She stopped in her tracks and then turned to look at her son.

"Kevin, this is Family Night. You see Tyrone ..."

"Ty."

"You see *Ty* everyday. This is *our* day, *my* day, and I did all of this cookin' for *you*, not some *nigger!*"

Kevin's face went blank. He had never used the 'N' word, and he had never heard his parents use it. Something fled him when it escaped his mother's mouth. He wanted to smash it like an overhead back into her, choke her on it, but he simply stared and began crying.

Kevin looked through his mom, at the rain falling heavier on the window. He remained silent—shuttled turkey, green beans, and mashed potatoes around his plate with the backside of his spoon, but nothing went into or left his mouth.

"Look, Kevin, your mother only meant that Tyrone is different, that's all. Nothing bad. I mean, he's black and that's okay, but he *is* different. They *are* different."

Kevin looked his father dead in the eyes, and then at his mother. "You mean the '*niggers*'?"

"Okay, Kevin. That's enough," his father said.

"But why stop now, Dad? It's not like they were brought here against their will, beaten, raped, murdered or anything. I mean, it's not like this country *owes* Black people anything for making it rich, making *White* people rich. It's not like they didn't help build this country or anything. As a matter of fact, Ty told me his ancestors were here one-hundred years before ours, or…"

"Kevin, I said I was sorry. I was just upset, and I've been so lonely since you spend so much time with Tyrone," she pleaded.

"Well, maybe you should apologize for being White, I mean, what would we be without *them*?"

Kevin's mom got up quietly from the table with tears in her eyes. He fell silent until she returned with dessert: a chocolate cake. Chocolate was his favorite.

"I made this for you. See? It's three-layers: dark, mocha, and chocolate chip. See, Kev-y, it's special."

Kevin looked at the cake, then at his father, at the cake, and then back at his mother. He pounded his hand into it, grabbed a fistful of chocolate on chocolate, smeared it onto his face, and then mashed it in his hair. His parents sat paralyzed as he continued darkening his face with the sweetness, matting his hair with thick, chocolate mud.

* * *

"Hi, Kev-y! You weren't answering your phone so I figured I'd drop by to bring you dinner. I hope you're hungry!"

Kevin stared at his mother's face. There were more lines than he remembered, and her skin had dulled, was made more eerie by the awkward mixture of hallway and apartment light.

"Well? Say something," she said, looking at him. She leaned in to kiss him; he did not pull away.

"Mom, why are you here?"

"Kevin, we have to end this. I miss you *so* much, and so does your father."

"Where is *he*?"

"He's in the car waiting for you to throw me out, but I told him this time would be different. It's different this time Kevin. *We're* different."

He wanted to believe her, but he still had not felt the words. He needed the apology to have as much weight as the insult on that Sunday, the Family Night when his world was shattered, or opened up; the day he realized that he was different, understood, through his parents' words, that he could not—as much as he wanted to—change his situation. He is White, which had only meant something because Ty is Black.

"Look, I brought triple-chocolate cake."

The phone fell from her ear to the floor as she handed Kevin the Tupperware. He opened the container as his stomach rumbled. She dipped her thumb-less hand into the cake and then rubbed it in her hair, graying and thinning.

...only get the bones? She asked me for a drink of water and I smiled and said politely, 'Here's 25cents, get up...

SWEET MELODY

I don't know if chairs have feelings. *I* didn't want you here in the first place. Not 'here' right next to me in the hallway, but 'here,' in my life again. You know what I mean? But if you could feel how I do right now…hell, maybe you *can* sense it. Look at you. All taped and patched up, almost like you know what it's like being hurt, too. I mean, you've been there all along, right? And for the life of me, I can*not* figure out how you came to be in Melody's possession. Maybe *you* know why she always does this kind of shit. Can't she just get it together? I mean, come on, she's twenty-two years old, and I don't think that she has a high school diploma or a GED, let alone ever held down a job. And the reality is, I'm not sure if she can stay with me much longer. Granted, she's only been here a week, but it's messing with my emotions a little bit, dealing with Mel, having to think about my father again, after, well…you know. I remember just before she first came to our house and all my father talked about was his 'Sweet Melody,' how I was going to have a little sister to watch over. But, enough is enough, right? I mean, it was 2:30 in the morning, and I was getting dressed to go bail her out of jail, *again*. I could hear her before I even got there, "Oh, Niecey, it wasn't my fault. I didn't do nothin', I swear! It's a misunderstandin' that's all." How lucky is she that her sister is an attorney, right? I *knew* I shouldn't have loaned her my car, and so *I* had to take a taxi. You should've seen her, sitting in the corner of the cell on that *dirty* floor. She had her legs crossed at the ankles, feigning like some innocent schoolgirl. You know what I mean? And I *know* that was my black mini-dress she was wearing, too. Her hair was a wreck, though, frizzed out on top like a black bird's nest. She looked like she had a rough night doing who knows what, but there *was* something about how her skin looked, all soft and buttery, like when she first came to stay with my father and me. I had always hoped that she could keep that, you know what I mean, and you know, somehow, with all that she's been through, she has. She stood when she saw me staring at her through the bars. Now, I can only imagine my expression, let alone what *she* saw on my face. We looked at each between the bars, in silence, and then the door slid open. Too much freedom for her, not enough for me. You know what I mean?

* * *

"Well, open the door."

"I can't find my key."

"You lost it, Melody? Already?"

"Maybe they didn't give it back to me at the police station. Cops steal stuff too you know."

"Apartment keys?"

"Well?"

"Here, take my key and open the door, please."

"What's *your* problem?"

"Mel, just open the door. These bags are getting heavy."

"So put 'em down then."

"I will as soon as you open the damn door. *You're* the one with no money who just *had* to stop at the store for a *few* things." I was so mad that I could've hit her, smacked her hard across her face, you know what I mean? But I remained calm. I simply brought the bags in and set them on the counter. I did *not* want to get into an argument with her because it was late, and I had to be at the firm by 8 A.M; that was in *two* hours. I still wanted to get a little bit of sleep if I could, you know? So, I simply said 'goodnight.'

"So, that's it, 'goodnight?'"

"What else do you want me to say that I haven't already said?"

"Well, I don't know, I guess I was just expectin' a little more of your hollerin' and preachin' and shit like usual."

"Look, Mel, I'm your sister, not your mother."

"Just stop right there, Niecey. Don't bring *her* up."

"I'm not. It's just that, like it or not, you *are* responsible for your own life now, and you've gotta get it together. Somehow, you've just got to hook your shit up."

"What if I don't? I mean...what if I can't?"

"Look, just get some rest. Some real sleep. Not 'in that chair in front of the TV' sleep. Okay?"

"But that's the only way I can keep my mind off all the fucked up stuff in my head."

"Well, maybe it's trying to tell you something. Maybe, you should just listen."

I think I slept for about forty-five minutes, an hour, *tops*! And when I got up, there she was, sleeping in you with the TV turned down low. The light from the TV made her look less hardened, lit up from the inside, you know what I mean? I started to wake her and tell her that I wanted to make an appointment for her to see my therapist. But then, I started feeling a little guilty, so I grabbed her flannel blanket from the couch and laid it over her.

The entire morning at work, I couldn't help it. I just felt so badly even though I didn't want to, but I did. I had to see her, talk to her about her life, you know what I mean? The more I thought about her, the madder I got. So, when I came home for lunch hoping to see her, the *last* thing I expected to find was her, with some strange men, lounging in my place, well on their way to lit up. One of them was grungy, all reclined back in you, hitting a joint, and I *know* casing my apartment. Mel and the other guy were sitting on the floor around the coffee table, practically on top of each other, shooting whisky. Of course, you *know* I flipped the fuck out.

"Melody, what the hell? I barely left for work and already all of this shit? You probably weren't even asleep when I left, were you? And who the hell are these guys? I told you I don't like strange people all up in my house!"

"Damn! We was just hangin' out, Niecey! Chill for a bit. It ain't about all of that!"

"Then what's it about, Mel? You tell me what IT'S all about. Huh?"

"Look, forget it. Let's go y'all. We can find someplace else to hang."

You know, they grabbed all of their stuff and walked right past me, didn't say a single word before Mel slammed the door extra hard. You know me, I paced around for a bit. I thought about calling back in to work, having my assistant reschedule the rest of my clients because my mind was racing, and I was all mad and anxious. But, instead, I tidied up a little which *always* helps me calm down, you know, swept and mopped the kitchen floor, vacuumed, dusted, ran the dishwasher, disinfected. I went back to work and the hours *flew* by. As a matter of fact, I barely remember the cases I worked on because I was so distracted thinking about what I was going to say to Mel when I got home. I kind of hoped she wouldn't be here, you know what I mean, or that if she was, she'd be passed out drunk and tired. It was quiet when I got off the elevator, except that I could hear Steve's TV blaring as usual from across the hall. When I opened my door, I looked around for anything missing, right? I spotted a letter from her on the coffee table, in her scribbly handwriting, on *my* pretty pink paper. She must've had this letter stored up in her for awhile; hell, knowing her, she probably even wrote it out before but never sent it. I don't know why I started crying when I read it. It just hit me so hard, you know? Maybe because she wrote about my father, and I guess, I'm so diligent about *not* thinking about him, that I couldn't do anything else but cry. Here. Listen:

Dear Niecey,

I think it's time for me to go. I know it's been a pain having me be here with you and I hope you know I appreciate it, <u>but</u> you have your own set ways too, Niecey. Every little thing has to be picked up and put in its own proper place or you go off! You always have to be in charge of everything, everything always has to go <u>your</u> way. Just like when we was kids, when I came to live with you and Daddy after my mom left me again. You was all nice and stuff in front of <u>him</u>, but I know you made him make me leave. I heard what you said to him that night when you and him was in the chair watching TV. Y'all thought I was sleep but I wasn't. I heard you tell Daddy to send me back, that you like things just the way they are, that you hate me. You said that you was going to cry all the time and stay in your room and not eat. You even told him you was going to kill yourself, Niecey! So, I left. I went back to my crazy-ass mom, til I couldn't take it no more. I would rather be in the streets, Niecey, on my own, taking care of my *own* business, instead of with her, *or* with you as far as that goes. I'm a survivor, Niecey! <u>A survivor!</u> I made it and I'm gonna keep right on makin' it. I didn't need you, her, or Daddy, that's why I didn't even go to his funeral. I know he hated me too, or he would've sent for me. But that was probably all you, huh? Being selfish, wanting him all to yourself. That's okay, though, 'cause now you're all alone, Niecey. That's right. <u>Alone</u>. And you might think I don't see it, but I do. I see how you try to keep everything inside, try to be all perfect, how you can't let stuff go. We are not that different.

Love,

Melody

Can you believe that? 'Love, Melody'? How can she write 'Love, Melody' when she thinks that I hate her, that *we* aren't that different? Well, I was even madder by then, but I had to go back to the office to pick up some briefs that I forgot to bring home, and you know why, so I left her a note, you know, just in case she returned while I was out.

Mel-

You don't know what the hell you're talking about.

Niecey

She didn't have many things to begin with, other than you and that blanket, so I figured she might return for more of mine, you know what I mean? I hoped that *whatever* she did, that *you'd* be gone when I came back from the office. And sure enough, as I was getting off of the elevator, I saw her sliding her box of stuff into the hall. I know she saw me even though she tried to play it off like she didn't.

"Where are you going?"

"Away, Niecey. Didn't you read the letter?" She wouldn't stop shuffling her few things around long enough to talk to me, and like *sooooo* many guilty girls I've seen waiting to be caught, you *know* she wouldn't even look me in the eyes.

"So, you must've read *my* note?" She shrugged her shoulders and made a little noise through her nose, and it *almost* sounded cute, you know?

"It's better this way. I need to be in control of my life again."

"'Again?'"

"Yeah, *again*."

When she said that last 'again,' she looked in my eyes, like someone on the stand trying to convince me of something, you know, a lie *or* the truth. In that moment, I could tell she *truly* felt she had been in control of her life once, you know? That *something* had been working for her, something that felt better than being here with me. I mean, maybe she *was* right about me, about us, how alike we are, and if that *is* the case, I *guess* I understand what she was doing, why she felt she had to leave. You're probably not going to like this part, but I had to inquire about you. I said 'What about that chair?'

103

"I can't take it now."

"Then when are you coming back for it?"

"I don't know."

"Well, I don't want it here, Mel. I'm just going to throw it out when you leave."

"You would, wouldn't you, Niecey? Just to spite me. I thought you'd *love* to have it after all the time you spent in it with Daddy. Shit, I couldn't never get a seat there. You *always* pushed me away, 'til I was gone, Niecey, and you could have him all for yourself again!"

"Look, Mel, I don't want it! Take it to the dumpster, leave it at the curb, do something with it. Just get it the hell out of here!" I didn't want to tell her, but I knew I might not ever see her again, so I did it. I told her about us: about me, you, and my father. "You don't know what he did to me in that chair, in front of the TV, with me on his lap. You don't know, Mel. I tried to protect you. I chased you away to save you! He would've done the same disgusting things to you. He would've destroyed your life, too!"

* * *

You remember that day when it all began, right? I was five, and I was getting ready for morning kindergarten. I went into the living room to watch TV until my father fixed me breakfast. I remember that I was watching *Sesame Street* and the letter of the day was 'U' and the number was '2.' I was sitting on the floor and my father brought in a bowl of my favorite, Honeycomb cereal, and when he handed it to me, it wobbled in my hand. He said, 'Don't spill any on the floor,' though I never do. He sat down on you and watched me eat my cereal like he always did before I went to school. 'Come here and let me fix your hair,' he said, so I got up and went to him with my bowl trying not to drop any cereal. He patted his leg, remember, and I sat on his lap eating my breakfast while he untwisted my old plaits and worked my hair into new, tight braids. He braided good for a man, too. When he finished, he hugged me close to his chest and I could really smell his cologne or whatever, and he was warm and I felt safe. But then, *you* know, his hand went underneath my dress, and then beneath my panties, and then he started touching me down there. You remember what he did next, don't you? I just continued eating my cereal, watching *Sesame Street,* and those words kept flashing on the screen: umbrella, ugly, us…umbrella, ugly, us. I had to sing along with Bert and Ernie inside my head to drown the sound of his heart beating louder and faster.

* * *

"No, Janiece. I don't believe you. You're lyin'. You're just tryin' to hurt me even more!"

"Why would I lie about something like this, Mel? I wouldn't lie about something like *this*."

"To hurt me. You'd lie to hurt me just like you did before!"

"No. It's the truth, Mel. The whole truth. I swear! That's why he went away to prison! *That's* why nobody told you where he was! That's where he died, too!"

I could tell by the look on her face that she didn't know what to say, what to think, whether to believe me or not. But then, the strangest thing happened. I felt myself get lighter, the muscles around my ribs seemed like they gave way, and I could *truly* breathe for the first time, you know what I mean? At that moment, I could sense Mel trying to see me differently, trying to see her own life as, …well, *maybe*, the gift that it was, you know what I mean, versus what she might have endured, what I had to live through. I mean, we both were angry, filled with sadness, lonely, you know, wondering why the people we loved seemed to only want to hurt us. She put on her sunglasses and stood still behind you, but I could tell she was crying.

"Niecey, how come you're just telling me all of this shit now, huh? Why didn't you tell me before, when it would've meant something?"

"I guess I didn't think it mattered. I mean, you were gone, lord knows where, and I was stuck where I was…and now, we are who we are already. Knowing that you weren't there kept me going, Mel…knowing that I had something to do with that meant I wasn't *all* bad, that I had done *something* good."

She took off her sunglasses and wiped her eyes with the back of her hand, then directly on you. She picked at a piece of your tape, and then we looked at each other over your back, breathed deeply, took each other in, you know what I mean? Like at the jail and when she first arrived at my father's house. I hoped that, *maybe*, she'd reconsider leaving now that she had all of the facts. She grabbed my hand and squeezed it tightly.

"I still have to leave, Niecey. I gotta get out of here." She let go of my hand and put her glasses back on. "But, I'll help you push this raggedy ol' thing out to the hall." She opened the door then grabbed your foot rest; I pushed hard on your back. We lifted and struggled with you through the door, trying to remember which angle got you in in the first place. Somehow, *both* of us stubbed our fingers between you and the doorframe, cursed your existence en route to the dumpster. But, then I saved you.

"Maybe we should burn it," Mel said, pushing the 'Down' button.

"I don't know, maybe somebody else can find some use for it."

"Who would want a fucked up chair like this? All taped up and faded? I mean, it's *green*."

I didn't know what to say, but when the elevator door opened, Steve stood there smiling.

"You ladies need some help?"

You *know*, I looked at Mel and she nodded for some reason. I held on, dug my fingers into your back, felt you surrender, you know what I mean? Then you slipped from my hands to the floor.

"Nah, that's okay, we got it."

"Yeah, thanks, though."

Steve walked away, and Mel and I stood with you in the elevator doorway with the door jammed open, stuck on *my* floor, disregarding anyone else's needs to move through the building, you know what I mean? Mel walked forward a little, backed you and me into the elevator, and as the door was almost closed…well, *you* know what she did. She stepped backwards into the hall and waved goodbye. Then, there *we* were, our reflection on the back of the steel door, kind of warped by its shiny surface, you know what I mean? I *swear* I saw my father in you, shimmering into view in the yellow light, and just as quickly, fading away.

...and buy your own!' Wrapped up in a hefty bag while Hollywood's all dressed in drag, when Mardi's over...

RAINCHECK

I haven't stolen anything in awhile, Steve thought, fumbling with his keys in front of his apartment door. In fact, it would be two years to the day, tomorrow, his thirty-fifth birthday, that he resolved to not steal again. Coincidentally, it would also be two years to the day, tomorrow, that he collected his income tax refunds, wiped out his savings to purchase a top of the line TV; a thirty-six inch, flat-screen, plasma TV he affectionately named, Artie. Steve squinted and looked through the peephole from outside his apartment, while trying, unsuccessfully, to unlock his door. His janitor-sized key chain clanked to the exposed, rectangular, tiled floor space left uncovered for a personalized welcome mat. He smiled as he caught the reflection of his brown, bald scalp glistening off of the floor, as he slowly bent to pick up his keys, banging his head on the doorknob. He laughed at himself as he thanked God for Fridays and after-work drink specials: two-for-one, top-shelf liquor until seven. He was special three times—six Stoli Vanils and tonic with lime twists. He guzzled them while sitting on the lonely stool at the end of Laleekey's Bar, a beach club on the Rehoboth, Delaware coast. It was on his way home and hardly anybody he worked with went there before midnight. The rolling tide, the crashing in, and the "shush" out also comforted him. He leaned his head against the door, tugged on his navy blue khakis, and regained his composure. He grabbed his canvas work bag, held it up like a prized but stinky fish, then laughed at the stupid logo of a multi-ethnic crowd of people trying to convey a sense of security with their "confident" faces and crossed arms. He hated this logo, but hated the slogan even more: *Sure Security – We Are Secure About Securing You!* "Yeah, right," he mumbled, flinging the bag over his shoulder. He steadied his key into the hole—turned—and then stumbled into his apartment.

Even drunk, Steve maintained his grand entry ritual. He tapped the light switch on the left wall and dropped his bag just inside of the door. A screwdriver and a security manual fell out, but he kept going. He liked pretending that he was a red carpet celebrity while walking the corridor to his living room. He checked his look in a mirror that he stole from a mom and pop antique shop in 'S'lower Delaware, after installing their security system. This time, instead of bowing to the crowd, he simply snatched the remote from the stolen phone stand, pointed and then puked, sprayed remnants of Buffalo wings, mini tacos, and deep-fried mozzarella sticks across his industrial-style carpet. He dropped to his knees and continued to wretch, looked up through tears that come from hard puking, blurring his vision even more than the vodka. The TV was not ON. He pointed the remote again, pressed the ON/OFF button harder, as if that would change the fact that he hadn't replaced the batteries. He crawled on his hands and knees to the wall, carefully avoiding chunks of partially digested bar food. He laughed again. "Fuckin' loser," he said, between laughs, tears, and dry heaves.

He placed his hands on the wall, began pulling himself up, off of the floor, and then stopped for a moment when his hands reached his TV. He ran his palms across the sleek, gray lines that separate the screen's high-tech glass from its hard black plastic and steel composite frame. He lightly pressed his hot cheek against the cool screen as the image of smiling people with big white teeth, hocking overnight tooth whitening potions, appeared. A line of drool oozed from his mouth, seemingly, into the mouths of the people on the screen. He resumed his climb until his right hand reached Command Center, the panel on top where the manual controls are hidden. He tried to get his left hand on top as well, and for a moment, the TV supported his entire six-foot two-inch, two-hundred plus pounds. From the depths of his alcohol-soaked stomach arose a wretch like no other, a pain that shot through the vertical center of his body, simultaneously, out the top of his head and through the tip of his spine. He involuntarily pulled down to counter his heaving and maintain his precarious balance. Somewhere in his clouded mind, he hoped the ripping sound he heard was something from him.

He woke up with his face mashed into the carpet, in vomit, glass, and blood from a small cut below his eye, on his left cheek. The TV's insides splayed across his legs and torso: broken glass, clear and opaque tubes, red, white, black, and yellow wires, and hints of copper. He blinked rapidly attempting to adjust his vision and memory. As he pushed himself up to his knees, he realized what had happened. Tears fell like sudden rain from his bloodshot eyes—this time, from sadness. He laid his face back down on the thin, soiled carpet.

* * *

Steve never missed his Channel Two Saturday morning TV lineup: home improvement, followed by art lessons: basket-weaving to quilting, rounded out by two solid hours of cooking shows.

He viewed these programs as self-improvement, the one thing he did for himself in the name of the future. He would nurse varying degrees of happy-hour hangover while relaxing in the recliner his neighbor, Janiece, gave him last year after her sister moved out, left it as partial payment for rent. It was old: synthetic leather, faded lime-green, patched up and feminine, but he didn't want to hurt her feelings by refusing. So, he had dragged the chair across the hall and grimaced on the other side of his door. Then, he sat in it for the first time, in front of his TV, and melted. She threw in a flannel blanket that he now keeps in the back of his SUV for the occasional solitary night at the beach. He had waited two months for a specific episode of the home improvement show to air, in which an old, New England barn was remodeled into an ultra-contemporary house. He had seen the preview for this show and was immediately reminded of the barn he played in when he was twelve. He and other little neighborhood kids commandeered the barn and, in the hay loft, re-enacted episodes of *Starsky & Hutch* (He was always HuggyBear.) and *The Superfriends* (He was always Aquaman.). The day they were finally caught, the red pickup truck barreling down the dirt road spinning up dust clouds, little Black children jumped and ran from every part of the barn. He, with a running start from the opposite end, jumped out of the two and a-half story hay loft. He felt real and hot and free— like he was flying. He has never felt that way since.

* * *

Steve tossed up yellow, white, and pink pieces of paper from the countertop drawer next to his refrigerator. He flicked sweat from his forehead as he examined then dismissed old receipts, paid and unpaid bills, and extra takeout napkins—a desperate search for the product insurance he purchased on his TV. He was sure he had secured the information, but in all of his precaution, he forgot where he stashed it. He shouted and pulled the drawer forward off of its hinges, upside down to the floor. Then he saw it: the yellowed envelope duct-taped to the underside of the drawer. He smiled and released it, reached inside for what would make his day: the insurance that would get him a new TV. His smile faded as he read the paper. Expired. June 1st. Last month.

* * *

He stared at the wall, the rectangle created by his TV keeping away dirt, dust, and smoke from Newports. He only indulged when he watched TV, one show after another, one cigarette after the next, inhaling every third drag in an attempt to lessen the detrimental effects. The clean outline on the grimy wall reminded him of his TV. He went to his spare bedroom; on the door in black marker was a sign: tv graveyard. He opened the door and walked slowly through the dark room. The lamp was on the other side where the only grounded wall socket was open. He felt around in darkness, kicking things that rattled, moving toward the light. He reached the lamp and clicked. The room lit softly, revealed strange shadows on the gray walls, jagged eruptions resembling Lego mountains. The space, larger than his actual bedroom, was filled with TVs: floor models from the Seventies, black and white GEs with large, hand-sized knobs, TVs in faux pine cabinets, and first generation color remote control sets—all in various states of disrepair. Some had been found, discarded at curbsides; a few had been left behind in apartments he moved into then quickly out of. Others were stolen and salvaged for parts. Picture tubes clanged on the floor as he shuffled maimed TVs from corner to corner, searching, first, for one in tact, and then, for one that worked. He uncovered a thirteen-inch, black and white set from the belly of an older, black-spray-painted floor model; the UHF dial was broken and it was antenna-less. He lifted the pitiful TV with one hand then tucked it under his opposite armpit. He wished there was enough of Artie to lay to rest there; he contemplated rescuing a few parts. The thought quickly made him nauseous.

Steve's *The Jeffersons* TV stand had been MIA for two years. He found it folded, tucked between his refrigerator and stove, behind dozens of brown paper bags, in the awkward space created by the appliances. He set up the stand directly below the clean shadow, plopped the pitiful TV in the center, on the picture of George and 'Ouise-y Jefferson. He retrieved a wire coat hanger and a pair of needle-nose pliers from the hall closet, unwound the hanger, and then looped it through the hole on top of the pitiful TV where the antenna had been. He pulled out the ON/ OFF knob and waited—nothing. He pressed the knob in and out again, this time, hearing a high-pitched tone. There was an orange glow that grew inside, visible through black slats on the back of the pitiful TV. A dot of bluish-white light erupted in the center of the small screen and grew concentrically outward until it filled the screen—white noise. He turned the UHF dial and tested each channel by positioning the wire hanger in all directions. Nothing. Then he used the needle-nose pliers to turn the VHF dial. Again, nothing. "Fuckin' piece of shit!" He tossed the pliers up and over his head. He needed a cigarette. He pat his pants pockets, found a matchbook from Laleekey's, then pulled a Newport from the hard pack. He put it between his lips, but hesitated before striking a match, placed the matchbook under the back left corner of the pitiful TV. He spun the UHF dial again and happened upon a crystal clear picture of Channel Six. "Sweet," he said, cigarette dangling, reaching for another book of matches.

The pitiful TV screen was barely visible through the increasingly dense cloud of menthol smoke. Steve tried adjusting the hanger-antenna, rocking the TV stand, propping one-side-two-sides-all-sides of the TV to no avail. No Channel Two. Still only Channel Six. He was about to push in the ON/OFF knob when a special news report pre-empted a teen magazine show segment on relationship abuse.

"We interrupt this program to bring you breaking news from the south suburbs. I'm Channel Six's Candy Jones and it has just been confirmed that a local man has died in a freak accident from wounds sustained when an electrical surge caused his TV to blow up and at him. The man was, reportedly, stabbed in the left eye by a three-inch glass shard and another severed a main artery in his neck. He apparently dialed 911 but could not clearly describe his location or condition, as he was suffocating in his own blood. EMS arrived on scene but was unable to save him. He was killed by his thirty-eight inch, flat-screen, plasma, MegaHighTron Definition FOTV 2005, hailed, most recently, as the best TV on the planet. The man's name is being withheld until his family can be notified. Unofficially, however, locals report that the man is a professor of engineering at the university, and that he might be originally from the South. We'll have more on this story in our later broadcast. This is Candy Jones, Channel Six News. We now rejoin our regularly scheduled program."

There were the usual gawkers at the scene dipping in and out of the camera-shot behind Candy Jones' umbrella, attempting to be seen on TV, even during such tragedy. However, Steve noticed a man in the background sitting on a step in the rain with his head bowed. He was dressed in a dark suit, dark tie, and light shirt—unintelligible color in black and white. The man had his head in his hands, and he shook it quickly, side to side. Steve had watched for the man to raise his head, look into the camera, be seen—but he never did. After a few minutes, he could no longer stand the disturbing teen talk. He pushed in the ON/OFF knob with his cigarette butt, gave it an extra mush with his thumb.

* * *

Steve always looked out the peephole before opening his door. He didn't like surprises. He opened the door then bent to get his newspaper. He heard Janiece's door open across the hall, saw her pink-polished toes peaking out of pale blue slippers.

"Hey, Steve."

"Hey, Janiece. How you doin' this morning?"

"I should be asking *you* that question."

"Why do you say *that*?"

"Well…the cut on your face…"

"Oh."

"…and I heard that loud noise comin' from your place last night *and* this morning. You got company?" Janiece moved her head to see into his apartment. He countered.

"Yeah, right. I've been having TV problems."

"All that noise? From *TV*?"

"Um, kinda. It sorta broke."

"Broke? How does a TV *break*?"

"Let's just say, the drink specials had me feelin' a little more special than I am."

"I think you're pretty special," said Janiece, moving closer to him. She placed her hand on his shoulder.

"I'm gonna look through the sale pages and head out later, see if I can find a new one."

She lightly squeezed his shoulder.

The moment of awkward silence was more the norm for him these days, especially around Janiece. He looked at her, waited for her to release his shoulder, again, not wanting to be rude. He smiled then went back into his apartment. Behind the closed door, through his peephole, he watched her bend down to get her paper, turn back to look at his door, and then step inside her apartment. He watched until the door closed— and a few seconds afterwards. He dumped the newspaper upside down onto the kitchen table, allowing the circulars to separate from the real news. He paced in the kitchen perusing electronics pages of mega-retail stores, mumbling about 'rip-offs' and 'bending-over' as he scanned prices that were worlds away from his current finances. He crumbled and tossed each circular into the pile of papers accumulating on his kitchen floor. He stared at the pitiful TV and then grabbed the small key ring with only his apartment keys from the phone stand. Smokes? Check. Lighter? Watch? Check. Wallet? Check. He snatched his jacket off the hook and headed out the door.

* * *

Steve was nearly out of cigarettes and his search for a TV in his price range was going nowhere. He had busted his routine of only smoking while watching TV, and found himself lighting up at every bus kiosk and outside of every store. He decided to get a cup of coffee and rethink his dilemma. He got off the Number Nine bus on Fifth Street, right outside of Café Coffé, the only nearby café that still carries Newports, and only because he services its security system under the table, for a discount price. He also gets free, unlimited refills. He lit his last cigarette then took a long, minty drag. The thought of going home to the pitiful TV, with only Channel Six to watch, made him grind his teeth between puffs. He tore open, to flatness, the green and white hard-pack, and then searched his pockets for a pen. He found a yellow highlighter in his inside jacket pocket, and on the bright, white underside of the cigarette pack, he frantically wrote, barely visible in the glare of the afternoon sun:

skip car insurance

skip car payment for month

max last card

overtime

payday loan ?

He exhaled his final drag, flicked the butt into the street, and then crammed the list into his pants' pocket. Through the cloud of smoke, he saw a lone salesclerk across the street, in the window of Stan's Pawn World. He had long, dusty-blonde dreadlocks, and was waving a red feather duster. Framed by the window, it was like watching a soda commercial, or one for a new cleaning product that is so good, it makes you dance. Steve smiled. He had never been in the store; he found pawn shops creepy. The salesclerk was dusting a few brightly lit TVs in the window, and as Steve approached Stan's, a Channel Six news teaser flashed across the TV nearest the door. The man in the dark suit walked in back of Candy Jones, head in hands, still shaking his head. His dark suit: brown.

"Welcome to Stan's Pawn World—I'm Kevin. Is there anything I can help you with?"

"Just looking," said Steve, averting the salesclerk's 'please buy something eyes.'

"Well, let me know if you have any questions." He grabbed a clipboard, stepped from behind the counter, and then walked in the opposite direction. Steve wandered the store among boomboxes, DVD players, used CDs, and VCRs. Then he spotted it, his dream TV: the MegaHighTron Definition FOTV 2005. He had only ever seen one in pictures. The salesclerk wandered over.

"Ah, yes. That's the. . ."

". . .the MegaHighTron Definition FOTV 2005," said Steve, smiling, nodding his head up and down. "What's the damage?"

"Oh, it's not for sale. You heard about that guy who got killed by *his* when it blew up?"

"Yeah, dude, that's some wild shit."

"Well, my boss, Stan..."

"There's a real Stan?"

"Yeah, he told me not to sell it 'til they find out what actually happened to that guy, you know, make sure it's not defective or nothin'."

"Makes sense," said Steve, shrugging.

"He's probably gonna pull it off the floor tonight or tomorrow anyway. We got a lot of other *sweet* TVs that just came in."

"I think I'll look around a little more."

"Take your time, Man," said the salesclerk, as he walked away putting on his headphones.

Steve strolled around the store but had his eyes on one thing, the MegaHighTron Definition FOTV 2005. He roamed to the back of the store, past the security door, then through the aisles, instinctively assessing the security cameras. He had already glanced the taping system behind the main counter when the salesclerk bent to dust some DVD players an aisle over.

"Thanks a lot," said Steve, heading for the door.

"Thanks for visiting Stan's Pawn…"

Steve was already out the door, heading back to Café Coffé for smokes.

* * *

"Hey, Steve. How did it go today?" asked Janiece, closing her mailbox.

He waved as he approached the bank of mailboxes next to the elevator.

"Well, I found a TV I want, but…"

"Let me guess, you want one of those TVs that killed that man, don't you?"

"I'm that obvious?" he said, closing his mailbox.

"When it comes to TV? Yup."

Steve flipped through his mail, stopped on an envelope, and smiled.

"Now, *that's* a smile," said Janiece. "You've been expecting that one?"

"Yeah, a letter from my aunt, my mom's sister. She's answering a big question for me."

The awkward silence returned.

"I'm going out with some of my homegirls later tonight, but if you want to grab something to eat before..."

"Um, well, I'm kinda startin' to feel it again from last night, and I can't even think about food right now. I'm just gonna chill, get some rest, you know, see how I feel when I wake up. Thanks, though."

"You're welcome, *Steven*. Maybe one of these times I'll be able to cash that raincheck you always give me. I gotta run to the salon to work some magic," she said, pointing to her scarf-wrapped head as she walked off.

* * *

Steve awoke from his five hour nap around ten o'clock at night. He hadn't eaten all day, and now that his body had finally settled from last night's 'bar-scapades,' he was ravenous. He raided his pantry, fridge, and freezer, gathered a smorgasbord of bachelor delights: beef vegetable soup from a can, microwave chicken fingers, microwave cheese burritos, ruffled potato chips con queso, and beers to wash it all down. He ate at his table for the first time in two years; he had always eaten in front of Artie. He began swigging from a bottle of Jack Daniels shortly after eating; he was feeling better: food plus a little hair of the dog. In his bedroom, he pulled out clothes from his dresser, his closet, and from under his bed, assembled the perfect night disguise: black sweat pants, black turtleneck, black knit hat, black shoes, black gloves, and black underwear. It was midnight when he heard Janiece and her homegirls leaving. He looked out his peephole hoping to see her, but only caught a glimpse of her fat friend, Relse. Back in his chair, in the dark, dressed completely in black, he nipped Jack Daniels and then turned on the pitiful TV—there was only snow and white noise. He sighed heavily then smacked the side of the pitiful TV for something, anything, to appear. There was a fuzzy update of the man killed by the MegaHighTron Definition FOTV 2005. The man in the brown suit was, again, sitting in the background, this time, on the dented hood of a car. His head was, still, in his hands, shaking. He whacked the TV one last time and then it blacked out.

It was one-thirty in the morning.

* * *

Steve drove the alley behind Stan's Pawn World with his headlights off. He wasn't sure at what moment he realized he'd been casing the store earlier in the day. He always checks out security features and alarms wherever he goes; it's part of his job that carries over into "real" life. He had noticed that the back door was a Kriegman 500, a basic security door that was about to be recalled due to a flaw that makes it easy to bust open. The release can be triggered with a solid kick corresponding to the height of the bar, about six inches from the lock. He had heard it through the security grapevine, which is a nice way of saying 'thieves.' He reared back, summoned all of his whisky-fueled energy, and then let loose on the door with a kick. Nothing.

He looked around, over his shoulder, and then kicked it a little higher; there was a "fwunt" and a release. He pried open the door and walked directly to the MegaHighTron Definition FOTV 2005, parted it from the wall by releasing the tabs on permanent tracks that lower the TV to the floor. He wrapped it in the flannel blanket, hoisted it into the back of his SUV, then sped off looking back only once. There was a re-broadcast of the New England barn remodel at 3 A.M.; he knew he could make it home in time.

* * *

Steve wiped his damp brow as he closed the door. He put away his keys, took off his jacket, but skipped the rest of his entry ritual. He slid the MegaHighTron Definition FOTV 2005 across the floor on the blanket, placed it directly in front of the pitiful TV, pushing them both against the wall. He wrapped the blanket around the base of the MegaHighTron Definition FOTV 2005. He scrambled around for his digital cable hookup, and then plugged the cord to an ultra-grounded power strip. He gathered supplies: beer, chips, cookies, cold pizza, cigarettes, and then arranged them on *The Jeffersons* TV stand, instead of the coffee table like he used to do with Artie. *"Well, we're movin' on u-up,"* he sang, smiling, pointing the remote control at the TV.

Steve sat mesmerized by the biggest, sharpest TV picture he had ever owned, drinking beer in a cloud of menthol smoke. At 2:55 in the morning, as the home improvement show was about to air, he heard Janiece's laugh in the hallway. He pressed MUTE, popped up, and the remote fell from his lap. At the door, he peered through the peephole and saw her on her cell phone, head thrown back, laughing as she opened her door. He turned to the MegaHighTron Definition FOTV 2005; the channel had changed when the remote hit the floor. The man in the brown suit was, this time, being interviewed by Channel Six's Candy Jones. He was no longer shaking his head and his hands were at his sides. Steve picked up the remote and pressed MUTE:

"... and what do you want others to know about the deceased?"

The man looked directly into the camera and said, *"I wish he had let others know him as well. All he ever wanted to do was truly see himself."*

Steve headed back to his door and stared through the peephole directly at Janiece's door. He turned and aimed the remote control. The TV made a strange sound—like an exhalation—then went dark. He placed the remote on the phone stand, glanced at his watch, and reached out for the doorknob.

It was 3:01.

*...who's gonna keep warm with beads? Mercy Me.
I ain't got none for you. Mercy Me. I wish I had
some for me.*

HIS BROWN SUIT

He's driving the back country roads around blind corners that weave and sharply turn in the night. The lightning bugs are standing still: neon hits of light buzzing in darkness. There is a low hum from nocturnal insects and the cold, lone telephone wire. It strikes him that the time has come for him to tell the truth, to look him in his warm, deep brown eyes, await the smile that melts him, take in his lips that he imagines are the perfect combination of soft and rough—tell him that he is the one who can make his life mean something, in a sense, give him life. Out of billions of people on the planet: multi-colored, multi-gendered, multi-modal—he is his non-local connection come local.

In the CD player, below the blue-green '1:30 A.M.,' an MP3 mix from him spins. They barely spoke of music outside of the occasional R & B show or satirical remark about the shame spiral of popular music. He pulls a joint from his shirt pocket then retrieves a lighter from the place between the seats where everything winds up. He lights it and inhales, thinks of how the meeting will go. Will he chicken out at the last minute as he has done so many times before? Will he resign himself to writing a letter that he'll never mail as he has done so many times before? Will he refuse to call so that he doesn't hear the sorrow and bleak optimism in his voice? He envisions this time differently—finally. He imagines his arms wide-open to him, unafraid of the thing that lingers between them, the magnetic pull of the universe, separation attempting to reconcile. He imagines, at last, feeling his full warmth, his heart, his body, and the heat they would generate together, which he has sometimes imagined being too much, consuming them both. He can see his head on his chest, nestled, centered in a wiry patch of curly brown hair, his heart beating fast, faster, then back to calm. He imagines the first time they consume each other.

It begins to rain. He cranks up the music, turns on the wipers, then inhales the last of the joint, ignoring the cherry eating away at the shared callous between his thumb and forefinger. He holds the smoke deep in his body, envisions it dancing through his organs, systems, skin, brain, awaiting the moment that he is lifted, when the high is visible in his eyes, reddened and dilated, and by the relaxed way he holds his jaw when his belly rises and falls from deep, diaphragmatic breathing. The heavy rain, the music, the wipers, his breathing and hastening pulse, create a soundtrack that threatens to overwhelm him. He blows out the stored smoke from his burning lungs, attempts to calm himself and gauge his emotions. The back country roads get more dangerous at night, even more so when wet.

Trees overhang the roads. He remembers, as a boy, biking on the roads to adventures that usually ended searching for water moccasins from the overpass at Andrews Lake. He gulps and realizes that he has been holding his breath, something he has done since he was four years-old to regain control over his body and any anxious situation. He recalls the many nights after hanging out with him as friends do; telling himself to keep breathing, control his heartbeat, remain steady as the idea of losing it, breaking down prematurely and telling him how he truly feels, would surely prompt him to parasitic guilt, which would definitely prompt him to suicidal thoughts. The CD begins to play from the beginning again. He turns down the music. The rain is softer.

He was fascinated by his mind. That's how it happened. And those brown eyes that returned him to 'boyish'. He imagines himself as he has numerous times, being enveloped by them, engulfed—smiling as his ultimate demise is validated. He opens all of the windows, feels the damp night cling to his skin. The wet tar smells of oil as rain brings it to life, struggles with it on the road's reflective black surface. He begins to cry as he realizes that the emotional weight of this declaration could mean they would never see each other again, that the burden of knowledge, spun eternally into the cosmos, would be too much for them, or maybe just him, to bear in the presence of his eyes. He rolls the windows up and unexpectedly sneezes, sprays yellowed snot onto the steering wheel and front window. He laughs, watches it roll down the inside front dash, gather with the intermittent raindrops towards the windshield wipers. He reaches under his seat, feels around and pulls out a flattened, almost empty roll of toilet paper. He cleans off the steering wheel, carefully avoids soiling his jacket sleeve, and then tosses the tissue on the passenger-side floor. He starts humming and then begins mouthing words until he is singing in full voice over the stereo. The rain has stopped and the headlights on the wet street reflect light into sharp corners on the Felton back roads. He wonders what lies in them, beyond them: roaming versions of Sasquatch, killer rabbits, snakes, and the horror of nothing. Blinding high-beams approach and he flicks his lights as a reminder to the other driver who immediately switches to low-beams. As they pass each other on the dark road, he wishes all communication was that easy.

His lips quiver. Sweat lingers on his forehead around his freshly-cut hairline. He grips the steering wheel in perfect three and nine and then inhales deeply. He exhales, opens the glove compartment and sifts through it, pulls out a yellow Wendy's napkin and places it on the seat. He looks up at the road then dives back into the glove compartment. He feels around through wet naps, paperclips, and mild taco sauce, retrieves a red Sharpie which he places between his lips cap-side out. He closes the glove compartment and momentarily refocuses on the road. He pulls off the marker's cap then puts it between his legs, and with the frayed marker, writes on the napkin in bleeding red ink: *I won't tell him*. He double underlines the '_I_'. He wipes sweat with the backside of his hand and then wipes his hand on his pants. He won't tell him because he is afraid of rejection from someone who has been so instrumental in his emotional development, helped him, if only in *his* mind, confront his feelings. In him he was able to reconnect to the person he buried so long ago. In him he was willing to trust. In his body he saw a mirror of his own. In his eyes he saw a rescue. He won't tell him because he is afraid that without him, he will no longer be able to see himself.

* * *

They met when he came into the electronics store five years ago on a Tuesday night. He had been there, on his only night off, subbing a shift for a friend. He told him he was there to buy a new TV, nothing but the top of the line, the lowest level of glare possible. He said that he hated catching glimpses of his reflection in TV sets, and that he was willing to pay for the best. He had shown him the finest: the MegaHighTron Definition FOTV 2000. He smiled when he saw the TV, and in that moment, he noticed his eyes light up, felt a stir from him, something deeper and more connected than he had ever known. He asked him what he liked to watch on such hi-tech TVs and discovered that they watched a lot of the same reality TV and science shows on PBS. He also found out that they played some of the same PlayStation games, and that the almost obsolete Tekken III was still their favorite. He had noticed that his shirt was from the local university; he said that he taught there in the engineering school. He had graduated from there four years ago with a psychology degree, and was working and doing 'personal research' which included writing, smoking weed, and drinking vodka. They exchanged cards: his, a business card from the university; his, one he made at home on his personal computer that read: 'person', with a phone number and an email address. When he was on his way out the door, wheeling a flatbed loaded with a big box, they traded smiles and waves goodbye.

* * *

He has to pee. He stops on the side of the road after an s-curve around Moore's Lake. At night, it's hard to see what lies between the trees, so he decides to "go" next to the car: droplets of piss spatter, bounce off of the road in the headlight light. Rain begins to fall again; he gets back into the car, crumbles the napkin, tosses it on the floor, and then starts to drive in the opposite direction. The music only reminds him of him, but he keeps it on. There is now a slight, creeping fog rising from the lake. He begins to cry but knows it would be best if he didn't tell him how he feels. Through his tears, sobs, and occasional tapping on the steering wheel, he begins to mutter "It's for the best. It's for the best." until he is yelling it, then singing it above the stereo. He drives faster. The curves seem more severe and they quickly appear from dark bends in the back roads. He furrows his thin, black brows, and in the rearview mirror, glimpses tension in his face. He drives even faster. The rain remains steady and hypnotic. He turns off the washer blades and allows rain to bounce from the windshield, tries to see in the small spaces between the drops as diversion from his deepening sadness, the sorrow of his not telling, which means, to some degree, his not living. He resumes the washer blades in time to see yellow, animal eyes reflecting in the road. He lays on the horn and they disappear; his heart is jump-started—racing.

He slows down then pulls onto the grass embankment. He cuts the stereo, engine, lights, and then reaches into his shirt pocket, pulls out another joint, twists it in his mouth. He lights it and smoke eases horizontally out of the slightly-lowered, passenger-side window. He drags off of the joint, holds it in, then stills himself, listens to the rain hit the car, identifies the different tones depending upon where it strikes: low and dull on the hood, hollow and bright on the trunk, tiny heartbeats on the roof. He lets go the smoke which fills the car in a gray haze, and then begins moving around inside listening for rain songs. He climbs to the backseat holding the joint in the air, juts his right ear against the window, then up against the roof. He squeezes his head into the back-window dashboard, takes a hit off the joint, and then draws a heart in the condensation on the back window. In reverse, inside the heart, he writes the letters 'F-r' then immediately wipes them out. He slides over and then to the front passenger's side, sits on the damp seat, drags on the joint as a few more raindrops trickle in, onto his face. He looks over at the driver's seat and imagines his body there, exhales in that direction, then waits for himself to appear, ghostly, in the thinning smoke. He does not. He presses the roach between his thumb and forefinger then places it onto his tongue, swallows, and puts his hand on the ignition key.

He pauses, breathes deeply, and then retrieves the crumbled napkin. Unfolding it, he reads aloud "I *will* tell him." He rotates the key, hits the lights and wipers, and K-turns out of the embankment to the other side of the road.

* * *

He is back on the road. He hates driving when it's raining. In high school Driver's Ed, he had learned of the perils of hydroplaning, which, secretly, frightened him so much that a gradual uneasiness sweeps through him when he's driving on wet roads. His anxiety increases as the result of an accident he had when he was home from college during Thanksgiving break. There was a mellow rain. He was returning from getting his young heart broken by the reality of unreciprocated love, and swears to this day that a man jumped out in front of him. He swerved to miss the man, but hit a large spot of oil sitting on top of the wet road. No one believed him. Sometimes he doesn't believe himself, but he can remember the feelings: how his chest hurt from his seatbelt and the bang into the steering wheel, how his mind raced, how his eyes burned from the blend of sweat and tears.

* * *

He is getting closer. The new found courage since his piss in the rain has mixed with his excited anxiety. He is sweating less; the idea of seeing him, feeling his heart beat against his, and sensing their eyes mingle, sends a quiet shiver through his body,—makes him smile. He stops lip-synching to the CD that has, yet again, restarted. He begins talking:

"Um, look. I wasn't gonna come but I had to see you—um, look. I couldn't wait to see you because there's something I have to tell you, something I—Hey, how *are* you? It's so good to see you, you look *great!* I...I...I like your haircut—What's up, dude? How have you been? I know you weren't expecting to see me so early in the morning, especially dressed in my favorite suit, but I couldn't sleep and I couldn't stop thinking about you so I had to come by and see you because I couldn't sleep because of what I have to tell you, so I hope you don't get mad and that you don't interrupt and that you let me say what I have needed to say to you for so long but it never seemed the right time—I need you—Yes, yes, that's it, 'I need you.'"

He yells and slams his hands on the steering wheel in rhythm. His voice mutates to a low moan and then to heavy methodic breathing. He fixes his eyes on the road, breathes deeper until his complete torso rises and falls. He looks down and is mesmerized by the solid grounding movement of his body. When he looks up, there are two, reflective yellow dots in the road, in his eyes, gazing at him—then impact, darkness, and a thud.

* * *

Once he told him a story about when he was a teenager growing up during the Sixties, in the South. He had been a nerdy kid with his nose buried in science and engineering books. It had been the hottest day of the warmest summer, and an invitation to a friend turned into an unplanned bash when some other guys from his tennis team showed up with liquor and beer. His parents were having an important party and he probably shouldn't have had people over, but under the pressure, he had said they could stay for a few hours. They got drunk in the record heat, and one of them got really rowdy and taunted him the entire time. He had been out by the pool and ran in when he heard loud noises and arguing. When he got inside, he went to help this black man who was being beaten senseless by the obnoxious guy. He and the guy got into a fight right next to the man who was bleeding and barely conscious. He had let the guy beat on *him* so that he wouldn't start again on the man—a family friend who had come to fix the AC. The man ended up dying; he said that he had, in a way, died too. It was the tears in his eyes when he told the story that first prompted them to touch each other; more than the timid chest to chest hugs of men, but full, warm-bodied closeness.

* * *

The car is stopped in the middle of the road, and a small deer's head is sticking from under the front end. The bumper is completely smashed; the hood has accordioned towards the passenger's side partly exposing the engine. There is a small crack beginning at the base of the windshield, in the wiper well, that gets thicker and branch-like as it spreads through the glass. He unfastens his seatbelt and massages his neck. He slides from behind the airbag, gets out of the car, and then pats himself down. The deer is making a strange, low, pleading noise that seems gargled with liquid. He walks to the front then looks at the deer, half-hidden under the dented car. A small pool of blood on the road by the deer's head is growing; its eyes are wide-open. The gentle rain has grown even quieter. At this moment he feels himself well up again. Now his pain consists of more than just his fear, his selfishness, and fond feelings; it seems to move away from him. He sits down next to the deer and tenderly places his hand on its neck; its eyes close, its pulse races; he begins to mimic its gargled pleading. He tilts his head to the side and then sticks out his tongue to catch the misty rain. Under the car, he sees that the deer's lower body is motionless, its heartbeat slowing, like his own. It opens its eyes, lets out a high-pitched wail that elicits one from him. He shivers. The CD is skipping: "...*mad world...mad world...mad*

world…mad world…mad world…mad world…mad world…
mad world…"

He leans into the car, gathers the deflated airbag into a ball, and then stuffs it between the dashboard and windshield. He gets in and turns the ignition key; the car stutters on the verge of turning over. He cranks the engine again and the car tentatively starts. He slowly backs up, careful not to cause the deer's body more harm. He pulls over to the side of the road incase another person is out at dusk, on his way to bliss or having his heart broken. He gets out of the car then stands over the deer's body, fingers entwined at his mouth. He decides to pull it off of the road into the bushes; he bends down and grabs its hind legs. As he starts dragging, he hears them crackle and notices they are severely broken. He leverages himself then begins the grueling task of getting the deer to the side of the road. Though young, it is heavy and immobile, and the combination of musk, anxiety, blood, and wetness makes him dry heave. The trail of blood shines as it mixes with the oily, wet road. Once there, he gathers a few soggy branches and leaves, sprinkles them across the deer's body. He stands silently over the makeshift grave with his hands at his side and then closes his eyes. The rain is heavier; drops hit hard as if punishment being maliciously thrown down on him. He runs back to his damaged car, gets in, takes out the CD, pauses, reinserts. It begins to play as he drives off, but then he ejects it, continues on in the night music framed by the memory of the deer's last gurgling breaths, and his own pounding head.

His heart is racing again. He tries to slow it and his breathing with some techniques he learned in yoga class, focusing his mind on light centers that flow along his spine to the outside top of his head. Calmer, he enters the quaint beach town and drives past the stately brick elementary school, and then First National Bank, its clock flipping to '4:00.' He looks for the big umber house on the left side of the street, just before he takes the right-hand turn by Morris' Market or, as the neighborhood kids like to call it, 'Bubbie's.' He drives Front Street and looks left at the little white church where he sometimes goes with him, and then, slowly drives back, deeper into the quiet, dead-ended town. Now, he is composed, even smiling. As he passes Fourth Street, he presses in the CD and then begins singing, tapping on the steering wheel and his leg. He thinks of the moment the way it would be: him in his face, looking deep into his eyes, unguarded, breathing with him, taking in his face as he told him everything; then he, with his heart and self open wide, would stretch out his arms, envelope him in his warmth, press his head on his shoulder. They would stand still—together.

When he turns left onto First Street, he sees light from the small, battery-op reading lamp through his living room window. He shuts off his headlights and rolls into the driveway next to his truck. He shivers and cuts the engine. He looks at the house for a moment, thinks about the Saturday they spent together painting it a fresher shade. He remembers how close he came to telling him that day in the glow of new yellow paint, and then he opens the car door. He rings the bell and waits, adjusts his suit and hacks into a bush. He knocks as hard as he can—softly—and waits. There is no answer. He knows he is home because of his truck, so he opts for the spare key hidden inside the decorative gray rock next to the bush where he spit. He opens the door and notices a strange, slightly electrical burning smell.

He flicks the light switch immediately inside of the door, but it doesn't come on. He walks toward the lamp and the smell gets thicker, mixed with something else…dampness. In the dim, early-morning light he sees glass shards and TV parts splayed across the floor, melted and burned, some even ashen. There are things attached to the TV by wires: a microwave, portable phone, his camping generator, CD clock radio, and a toaster—all in various stages of meltdown. He is in the chair directly in front of where the TV used to be. His shirt is blood-drenched except for a small, white rectangle across his belly where the remote must've been before it fell to the floor. There is a big cut along the right side of his neck and a large piece of glass lodged in his eye. He walks even closer, hoping part of him will move. There is a white envelope addressed to him, splattered with blood, at the foot of his chair. He sinks down to the floor then lets out the breath he has been holding ever since he took in the odor. He holds the envelope to his chest then crumbles it into his pants' pocket. There is a loud crack of thunder that makes him jump to his feet, followed by a bolt of lightning that harshly lights their bodies in gray and pale blue. The rain begins to fall again—hard. He walks outside and looks up. He's crying but doesn't want to feel his tears, so he lets the rain hit his face. He sits in his car, starts and revs the engine like he could immediately zoom away. He gets out, sits on the dented hood, covers his face with his hands then shakes his head. The CD resumes.

His brown suit, heavy and soggy, looks almost black.

Mad World

Canons scream at the tops of their lungs and pierce

the ears of the horrible world with no mercy. A head

bashes a wall and the wall begins to bleed and cry but

no one comes by to give. Voodoo girls and Christian

boys make love and sex and chocolate cakes that wind

up twisted, on the streets, with no icing. Mercy Me.

I ain't got none for you. Mercy Me. I ain't got none for you.

Chicken pox and pots of chicken, Colonel says,

"They're finger lickin'!" but what about those who

only get the bones? She asked me for a drink of water

and I smiled and said politely, "Here's 25cents, get up

and buy your own!" Wrapped up in a hefty bag while

Hollywood's all dressed in drag, when Mardi's over,

who's gonna keep warm with beads? Mercy Me.

I ain't got none for you. Mercy Me. I wish I had some for me.

www.ingramcontent.com/pod-product-compliance
Lightning Source LLC
Chambersburg PA
CBHW021018180626
46814CB00003B/1343